"I don't need your pity or your help!"

Stuart snarled. "Don't touch me, Andrea. I can manage. Remember that...."

Searing desperation engulfed Andrea as she wondered how they could continue their marriage in this way. They would destroy each other if it went on like this. Was any subject safe between them now?

"You never listen to me!" she flared in one last desperate appeal to move him. "You only believe what you want to believe. I don't know why, but you want to believe that I'm like Barbara—that I've cheated you as she did. Well, I haven't! And I'm sick of your accusations and your hatred and contempt. I can't go on living with you...."

To Begin Again

by

JAN MacLEAN

Harlequin Books

TORONTO • LONDON • NEW YORK • AMSTERDAM
SYDNEY • HAMBURG • PARIS

Original hardcover edition published in 1978
by Mills & Boon Limited

ISBN 0-373-02210-7

Harlequin edition published November 1978

PRINTED IN U.S.A.

CHAPTER ONE

THROUGH her bedroom window Andrea MacKinlay stared unseeingly at the magnificent vista of snow-covered mountains. She leaned her forehead against the cold pane, one slim hand clenched on the dull brown curtains.

Nothing had gone right since Ronald Martin had come home to spend a few days with his parents, she thought wearily. The job had been bad enough before that, but now that she had to spend half her time avoiding him, the whole thing was becoming intolerable. In her mind's eye she could see him as clearly as if he were standing in front of her . . . conventionally handsome face, although a trifle weak-chinned in profile, sleek blond hair, a slim body immaculately attired in the latest of male fashions. A rising young executive in a Vancouver manufacturing firm, he was extremely self-assured, a self-assurance which seemed to take for granted that she, Andrea, would be so flattered by his attentions that she would fall immediately into his arms. When she had shown a shrinking distaste rather than delighted acquiescence, he had assumed, as he coarsely put it, that she was playing 'hard to get', and had doubled his efforts. Her only comfort was that he would be gone in four more days; the time couldn't go fast enough as far as she was concerned.

She looked at her watch. It was after five o'clock and Mrs Martin would be wanting her afternoon tea. She'd better go. If only she could shake off this mood of foreboding, a mood as grey and heavy as the sullen sky over the mountains . . .

Behind her the door opened quietly, and, as quietly, closed. Absorbed in her thoughts, Andrea did not hear it. She moved to the dresser, leaning forward to brush her hair in the mirror. In its shadowy depths something moved.

Her heart pounding, she whirled to face the unknown

5

menace, the hairbrush a ridiculously futile weapon.

'Oh, Ronald,' she whispered shakily, her first reaction one of relief that it was only he, 'how you frightened me!'

Weak-kneed from the shock, she was a fraction too slow in guessing his intentions. Before she could move away, his arms were tight around her and she was being kissed with a wet-lipped fervour that repulsed her.

She fought frantically, but he was stronger than his appearance would suggest. Feeling as though she would faint if she didn't get air, Andrea broke free of his kiss. 'Let me go, Ronald,' she gasped. 'Let me go, or I'll scream!'

He laughed and she could smell the liquor on his breath —so that was what had given him the courage to come up to her room! He tightened his grip in spite of her struggles, and his lips again fastened themselves on hers.

A voice as cold and cutting as ice spoke from the doorway. 'Miss MacKinlay! Will you kindly explain to me what's going on here?'

In no hurry to release the trembling girl in his arms, Ronald Martin turned to face his mother. There was a foolish smirk on his face. 'I suppose I shouldn't be here, Mother,' he said, his manner a travesty of an apology. 'But when a girl as pretty as Andrea invites a fellow to her room, what's he supposed to do?'

'That's not true!' Andrea spat in furious denial. 'I didn't invite you in—you sneaked in behind my back. I'm so glad you came, Mrs Martin, I didn't know what I was going to do.'

There was an electric silence. Eleanor Martin, cool, elegant, and imperious in cashmere and pearls, gave Andrea a look of the purest dislike. 'Are you calling my son a liar, Miss MacKinlay?'

Aghast, the girl stared at her employer. 'I didn't invite him into my room,' she repeated, spreading her hands in helpless appeal. Mrs Martin had never been overly cordial, but this open antipathy made a shiver go down Andrea's spine.

'So you *are* calling him a liar?' Mrs Martin persisted, her eyes glittering with spite.

Quite suddenly Andrea had had enough. Warm reviving anger poured through her veins. 'Yes, I am calling him a liar,' she said steadily. 'Not only a liar, but a bully and a coward.'

'That will do, Miss MacKinlay.'

'No, it won't,' Andrea cried, in a glorious flood of freedom releasing words that had been banked up for days. 'Your precious son has made my life a perfect misery ever since he came. He thought I'd be too afraid of losing my job to say anything. And now that he's been caught in action, he has to hide behind his mother's skirts!'

Shaking with fury, Mrs Martin said, 'You will leave this house immediately. You're dismissed!'

'You can't dismiss me—I resign,' Andrea declared recklessly. 'And believe me, I won't be able to leave your house fast enough. Now if you would both excuse me, I have to pack.'

Mrs Martin had met her match. She marched out of the room, her son slouching behind her, both of them preferring to ignore the contempt blazing in Andrea's brown eyes.

From beneath the bed the girl hauled out the old leather suitcase that had belonged to her father, and began throwing in her belongings with a careless abandon quite unlike her usual neat-fingered efficiency. She snapped it shut, pulled on her outdoor clothes and gave one last unregretful look around the bare little room. Then, her cheeks still flushed with temper, she marched down the stairs and out of the front door, shutting it with unnecessary vigour.

The cold March air struck clean and pure after the ugly scene she had just participated in, and gratefully she inhaled its crispness. She hurried down the lane in the direction of the crossroads; the only bus of the day would pass through at six-fifteen, and she had to be on it. Because her brain still seemed incapable of logical thought, she realised she would have to make some concrete plans on the bus. But whatever uncertainties the future might hold, she was at least free of that dreadful job and those hateful people!

She turned the last corner to the crossroads and slowed

down, panting. Then her attention was caught by a flicker of movement to her left. In stricken silence she watched the bus tail-lights disappear around the bend with a final mocking gleam of red.

Horrified, Andrea stood rooted to the spot. She couldn't have missed it, she simply couldn't! It was only a little after six, and the bus never left before six-fifteen. She pushed her coat sleeve above her wrist to check her watch, and saw with a sinking heart that it still said five past six, just as it had several minutes ago. She must have forgotten to wind it. Shivering, she pulled her gloves back on, and tried to take stock of her situation.

She was standing on the verge of a country road, a small still figure quite alone in the bleak winter landscape. The road, long and lonely, was bordered by low brush and scattered trees on either side, white images still covered with yesterday's snow. Behind Andrea the mountains loomed black in the gloom, for it was rapidly becoming dark. The birds were silent in the trees, and not a single star pierced the heavy leaden sky.

Andrew shivered again, as the full enormity of her plight began to dawn on her. What on earth was she to do now? She looked back the way she had come, but there was no one in sight, and the gaunt peaks gave her no comfort; in the other direction the rumble of the bus had long since faded, leaving utter silence pressing against her ears.

Her eyes flitted nervously along the edge of the road. Cynthia, her aunt, had always accused her of having too much imagination, and in the gathering dusk it was only too easy to people the dark shadows under the trees with phantoms ... or, as would be more likely, with a hungry wildcat or even a pack of wolves. Surely the grizzlies would still be in hibernation ...

Perhaps it was the memory of Cynthia, with her cold blue eyes and her ramrod-stiff spine, that made Andrea straighten her shoulders and defiantly lift her chin. She must not panic. After all, it was really quite simple. Just a few miles down the road was the resort town of Valleyfield. She would probably get a lift before she got there, but if not she was entirely capable of walking the whole distance. And she could stay the night in Valleyfield and make connections with the bus to Calgary tomorrow.

When she reached this point in her decision, the thought that she had pushed to the back of her mind abruptly and unpleasantly surfaced and a little voice jeered, 'Why are you going to Calgary, Andrea? Are you going back east to Cynthia's empty house? She's away, surely you remember that. But then, if you don't go there, where else can you go?'

In spite of her best intentions, Andrea's lip quivered. Even when her aunt and the servants were in residence, the girl hated that house, hated its stark and ugly furniture, its grey walls and black carpets, its garishly modern paintings. To be in it alone would be more than she could stand. Yet where else could she go?

One thing was certain; she would never return to the Martins' house, from which she had so precipitately fled an hour ago. So it would have to be Cynthia's.

A snowflake brushed her cheek and in sudden alarm she looked up at the sky. Another flake drifted by, and another, and another, with a deceptive slowness that frightened her, wise as she was in the way of Canadian winters. Thank goodness she had had the sense to put on her thick winter coat and her fur hat and mittens! She picked up her case and began to walk down the road, her boots crunching in the frozen snow.

An hour later she slowed down to get her breath, changing her case to the other hand, for it seemed to be getting heavier by the minute. It was now pitch dark. The snow had closed in on her, obscuring her surroundings and muffling the sound of her own footsteps; in vain her ears strained for the noise of an approaching vehicle. All sensible people were home tonight, she thought grimly, quickening her pace, home where they belonged. In a wave of depression she wondered if she would ever have a home again, a place where she would be welcomed and loved and wanted. When her parents had been killed eleven years ago, all the warmth and happiness she had known had died with them. In vivid detail she could recall the old farm-house, nestled in the gentle hills of the Margaree valley in farway Cape Breton. Roses and honeysuckle had climbed over its grey stone walls, the hens had clucked and scratched in the yard around it, dogs and cats and kittens had casually wandered in and out. And, far more important, it had overflowed with happiness and laughter, because her parents had deeply loved each other and their tiny dark-haired daughter.

With a sharp sigh Andrea came back to reality. Those days were gone, gone for ever, and instead of longing for the past, she'd better start coping with the present. A wind had sprung up, driving the snowflakes against her cold cheeks and down the collar of her coat; it was becoming an effort to put one foot ahead of the other and twice she nearly stumbled off the edge of the road, confused by the whirling curtains of snow. She struggled on, fear nibbling at the edges of her self-control, her breath coming in harsh gasps. Now that it was too late, she realised she should have swallowed her pride and anger, and gone back to the Martins'—she must have been crazy to have started for the bus with a blizzard on the way.

But even as she thought this, she remembered Ronald's body crushing her against the wall, his hot breath fanning her cheek, his lips bruising hers. The girl shuddered with more than the cold, knowing full well she couldn't have returned there, not if it was the last thing she did.

To stop these rather ominous words sounding in her brain, and to take her mind off her weariness, she instead concentrated on the thought that with every footstep she was increasing the distance between her and the odious Ronald. Nor, if she were to be honest, would she miss his mother. Wife of a prominent, though now retired, barrister, Eleanor Martin had long been a friend of Cynthia's, and it was through her aunt that Andrea had obtained the job; she had been in no position to be choosy.

It had not been a rewarding experience either emotionally or financially. Mrs Martin had lavished money on her beloved son and daughter, on herself, and on her luxuri-

ously appointed home, but as far as her staff were concerned she had pinched pennies with miserly efficiency.
Andrea had been hired, innocuously enough, as a companion. Two weeks after she arrived, the maid had left, so
Andrea had taken over her duties. Furthermore whenever
the cook, a buxom lady of uncertain temper, flew into one
of her tantrums, the girl found herself delegated to produce
gourmet meals that would tempt the fickle palate of the
retired barrister.

It really sounded like something out of the Victorian era,
Andrea mused, as she trudged along the road, and until
today she had felt powerless to escape. Apart from any
other considerations, she had been too busy to look for
another position. If Ronald Martin had not come home last
week to spend a few days with his doting parents, she
would be there yet. Perhaps after all, she had reason to be
grateful to him, although when she recalled how she had
been accused by his mother of trying to seduce him, she
was filled with chagrin.

The trouble was, Cynthia would unquestionably side
with her friend Eleanor's story rather than her niece's, so
Andrea would be in double disgrace. It really wasn't fair . . .

Even if Andrea's attention had been on the road, she
probably wouldn't have seen the patch of ice so treacher-
ously hidden beneath the new-fallen snow. Her left heel
slipped, and she lost her balance, falling sideways and
wrenching her knee with a pain so sharp that she cried out.
She collapsed into a snowdrift, fighting back tears of
weakness. It would be the left knee, of course—the old
injury of two years ago. As her mind shied away from that
bitter memory, she struggled to her feet, tentatively putting her weight on the knee. If she was careful it would
hold her, she decided, and started off again, limping badly,
and trying desperately to subdue the fear that threatened
to destroy her self-control. Her progress was becoming
slower and slower, and although she longed to rest, she
had heard enough stories of travellers lost in snowstorms
to know that if she once stopped, she would never get up
again. Almost imperceptibly she drifted into a stupor of

exhaustion, no longer fully aware of where she was going or why, only certain one foot had to go in front of the other.

She had wavered into the middle of the road, head bowed against the wind, when from nowhere bright yellow headlights transfixed her in their glare. Trapped in the light like a terrified animal, she was totally unable to move. Dumbly she watched as the vehicle came closer and closer. It skidded sideways and finally shuddered to a halt a scant few inches from her motionless body.

A man got out and reached her in three long-legged strides. Grabbing her by the shoulders, he shook her like a puppy. 'You stupid little idiot! Don't you realise how close I came to killing you? I didn't even see you until I was nearly on top of you. What the hell are you doing wandering around after dark in the middle of a snowstorm?'

Her mind seemed to have gone as numb as her body. She gazed up into his eyes, deep wells of angry grey, in which she felt herself drowning, drowning, drowning . . . her head fell forward against his jacket and her body went limp in his arms.

A trickle of fiery liquid was burning its way down her throat. Feeling as though it would choke her, Andrea sputtered and coughed, moving her head away in mute protest from the flask held against her lips.

'Come on, drink up,' the stranger said crisply. 'It's only brandy.'

Argument was obviously useless. Obediently the girl swallowed another mouthful, grateful for the warm glow that spread through her limbs. The interior of the vehicle was blessedly warm too, and the man had tucked a thick fur rug about her legs. Unconsciously he gave a deep sigh of relief and relaxed against his hard shoulder.

'Feeling better?' he said impersonally.

She nodded wordlessly.

'Good. I'll suspend further questions until we get home. You'd better pray it doesn't get any worse or we may spend the night in the jeep.'

Not the sort of man who exuded comfort and reassurance, thought Andrea, recovering a vestige of her sense of humour. Yet oddly enough, she was no longer afraid.

The jeep moved slowly forward in second gear, the wipers making only a slight impression on the flurries of white that blew towards the windshield. In the dim light from the dash, Andrea studied the face of her rescuer.

He was intent upon the road, a faint frown between his brows, although his hands were loose and relaxed on the wheel. They were very attractive hands, the girl decided, lean and well kept, with a latent strength in the long fingers. The man was wearing heavy leather boots, his dungarees tucked into the top of them, and a suede jacket with a sheepskin lining, open at the neck to show a turtle-neck sweater that matched the smoky grey of his eyes. His face, too, was lean, with the year-round tan of a man who spent much time outdoors. It was difficult to guess his age—perhaps in the mid-thirties, since there were threads of silver in the thick black hair that was spangled with moisture from the melting snow. He looked tough and resourceful, well able to cope with life in a land that was often hard and cruel. Did that account for her complete absence of fear? But she knew it was more than a mere absence of fear. She was aware of an almost childlike sense of trust in this stranger, and trust was an emotion she had buried for years; it had been a luxury she could not afford. Its reappearance in such unlikely circumstances filled her with wonder.

'Do I pass?' he asked abruptly.

She blushed, for she had assumed he was concentrating on the driving and would not notice her somewhat prolonged scrutiny. 'I'm sorry,' she murmured. 'I must have left my manners back there in the snow. I haven't even thanked you for rescuing me, Mr—— but I don't even know your name?'

'Trent, Stuart Trent. And yours?'

'Andrea MacKinlay.'

'We'll forgo shaking hands, Miss MacKinlay, I don't want us both to end up in the ditch. We're nearly there anyway.'

'There' must be their destination. Curiosity stirred in

her, while her vivid imagination supplied him with a rustic log cabin hewn from the wilderness, deep in the hills.

He peered through the glass and gave a grunt of satisfaction. 'Here's the driveway. I was beginning to think I might have missed it. Hold on.'

Swinging the wheel sharply, he accelerated up a steep slope and she fell against his shoulder, suppressing a gasp of alarm as the jeep slewed on the ice. With a skill she had to admire he guided the vehicle along a narrow lane bordered by stands of birches, their pale trunks wraithlike in the snow. Someone had marked the lane with a series of upright poles, each topped by a strand of bright orange plastic; as the storm whirled and blew, these were the only signposts, and at times the jeep slowed to a crawl while Stuart Trent patiently searched for the next one. This snail-like progress continued for nearly half an hour; Andrea had completely lost her sense of direction, but divined she was being carried further and further away from such meagre civilisation as Valleyfield represented. There were no lights, no houses, no telephone poles—only darkness and blowing snow surrounded the tiny island of warmth and safety that was the jeep.

For the first time her strange sense of confidence in Stuart Trent wavered. She remembered Ronald Martin and wondered with a sickening lurch of her heart if she had jumped from the proverbial frying pan into the fire. She darted a quick glance at her rescuer, now noticing the harsh lines that grooved his cheeks, the hint of sensuality in his chiselled lips, the virility of that hawklike profile; when she had fainted into his arms, there had been a brief instant of awareness of their hard, strong clasp. And where-ever she was being taken, it was certain there would be no escape, not until the blizzard had exhausted its fury. She was completely at his mercy.

The jeep shuddered up an incline, its tyres fighting for traction. She closed her eyes in sudden panic, her mittened fingers tensely clenched in her lap.

Then a hand rested on hers and Stuart Trent's deep voice said gently, 'Don't look so worried. I'm not abducting you,

you know. My housekeeper will be delighted to see you, she pines for female company in the winters. Just relax, we'll be there in five minutes.'

Andrea looked up at him, blinking back tears of relief. A smile lifted the soft curve of her lips. How well he had understood her fears, and how tactfully he had dispensed with them!

He put his hand back on the wheel to guide the jeep round one last corner. A cluster of gold lights shone through the blackness, incredibly welcoming. Unconsciously she expelled her breath in a tiny sigh. The jeep ground to a halt.

'Here we are. Sit tight while I get your case, then I'll let you out.'

As she waited Andrea gained a confused impression of a sprawling house of stone and cedar, its two bow windows brightly lit. That part of her that was starved and lonely for a place and people to call her own yearned towards the golden glow of lamplight; was she being fanciful to think that here she might find more than simply a haven from the storm? Then her spirits sank. Such a house, so different from the log cabin she had imagined, must have not only a housekeeper but a wife, an elegant and beautiful creature fit to be the mate of the handsome Stuart Trent. Nervously she wondered what his wife would think of him arriving late at night with an unknown and bedraggled stray. As he opened her door she stammered, 'Your wife? She'll think——'

His features hardened. 'I have no wife,' he snapped. 'If you're worried about the proprieties Mrs Hamilton, the housekeeper I mentioned, will look after you. We get very few visitors, so you'll be quite a novelty. And I've already told you to stop looking so scared. We won't eat you.'

I'm not so sure about that, she mentally retorted. No wonder you haven't got a wife, if you're this disagreeable all the time!

She slid down from the jeep, and the full force of the storm struck her, so that she staggered. His arm came taut around her, and she was annoyed at herself for needing its support. Buffeted by the gale and nearly blinded by the driving snow, they fought their way towards the huge front door, Andrea trying hard to disguise her limp. Somewhere in the house a dog was barking loudly and insistently. All Andrea's previous confidence fled, leaving her afraid, afraid of entering the home of the angry stranger. It was as though with true feminine intuition she knew her life would never be the same again . . .

The door opened. She blinked in the flood of light at the plump grey-haired woman who ushered them in, talking continually as she did so. 'Oh, goodness, Mr Stuart, sir, I was beginning to get worried. What a dreadful night! Has there been an accident? Come in, my dear, come in.'

This last was addressed to Andrea, who found herself standing in a vast hallway, its floor of gleaming parquet. Shivering with reaction and fatigue, she wondered with a strange sense of detachment whether she was going to faint again, for the paintings on the wall were dipping and swaying in a most alarming fashion, neither could her eyes seem to focus on the two immense dogs greeting their master in rough-tongued affection. From a long way away came Stuart Trent's deep, and already familiar, voice.

'The young lady was lost in the snow, Maggie. I'll take her up to the green room, if you wouldn't mind heating some of your delicious soup and bringing it up to her.'

Clucking in concern like a mother hen, Mrs Hamilton disappeared. Before the girl realised his intention, Stuart Trent had swung her up into his arms with a smoothly muscled expertise that made a mockery of her own feeble strength. Too exhausted to put up even a token protest, she let her head flop against his chest, conscious only of the utter security of his embrace. In silence they went up a short flight of stairs, along another hallway to a beautifully proportioned bedroom, decorated in restful shades of pale green and rose. Andrea was settled in a velvet-covered armchair with a gentleness oddly at variance with his cold, withdrawn features. Then, to her consternation, she saw that the man was kneeling down in front of her, fumbling with the zippers of her knee-high boots.

'I can manage,' she stammered, embarrassment bringing a trace of colour to her pale cheeks.

He looked up, a glint of humour softening the austere lines of his face. 'Don't argue,' he said. 'You're at the end of your tether, and you know it.' He slid the boots from her feet, and chafed her cold toes between his fingers. 'That ought to feel better.' Then he undid her coat, lifted her out of it, and removed her wet hat and mittens. She submitted as a tired child would, obscurely comforted by his ministrations; they seemed to contradict the anger he could unleash easily. But all too soon she found out that her respite was a brief one.

'I'll light the fire,' he said, 'and turn on the bath water. Maggie will unpack your clothes for you, and bring you something to eat. Bed after that—we'll talk in the morning. Tomorrow if the snow's stopped I must get a doctor to look at that knee of yours, too.'

She shrank back into her chair, the shy smile wiped from her face. 'That won't be necessary. It's an old injury which left the knee permanently weak. There's nothing a doctor can do for it.' The bleak words seemed to echo in her head; she bit her lip, determined not to cry in front of him. That the injury of two years ago had altered her life catastrophically was not something he needed to know. If only she could forget those bitter memories herself . . .

The man's grey eyes were fastened on her white face, his expression inscrutable. 'I see,' he said slowly. 'Well, that's something we can discuss in the morning. In the meantime I'd better phone your home and let them know you're all right.'

For Andrea, her nerves already stretched to the breaking point, this was the final straw. Her voice ragged with strain, she cried, 'There's no one to phone, no one! Please, just go away and leave me alone.'

His eyes narrowed in suspicion. 'Don't be silly, there must be someone,' he retorted. 'You can't have just appeared out of nowhere. Besides, you must have had some destination in mind. Where were you going?'

'That's really none of your business.'

'As I'm probably responsible for saving your life, I would
have thought it was very much my business. However, as
you obviously don't agree, we'll drop it for now. Here
comes Maggie, so I'll leave you. Sleep well, my mysterious
Miss MacKinlay. Perhaps a good night's sleep will loosen
that very uncommunicative tongue of yours.'

Her throat aching with unshed tears, she watched him
give her a mocking bow before he left the room. He had
saved her life, there was no question of it, and she had
barely thanked him. Moreover, she was a guest in his home
and had repaid his hospitality by being thoroughly rude to
him.

Her distress must have shown, for Maggie Hamilton,
after one look at her, capably took control. In no time at
all Andrea was bathed, fed, and in bed, her feet curled over
the hot water bottle, a thick eiderdown pulled up to her
chin. Watching the flames flicker in the hearth, she drifted
off to sleep.

An hour later the door opened quietly. Stuart Trent
entered, his footsteps soundless on the thick carpet. He
raked up the fire, carefully replacing the guard, then in the
glow of the coals studied the face of the girl sleeping in the
big four-poster bed. Her hair, a dark brown warmly tinted
with auburn, fell in soft waves to her shoulders, and
framed a delicate-featured face whose mouth was softly
curved in sleep yet whose pointed chin showed consider-
able firmness for one so young. Her skin was clear and
luminous, though smudged with weariness under her eyes,
while the firelight cast shadows beneath her high cheekbones. She stirred a little, and as quietly as he had entered,
the man left, closing the door behind him.

When Andrea awoke the next morning she lay still for a
few moments, bewildered by the unfamiliar surroundings,
before the events of the previous day rushed back into her
consciousness, and she remembered exactly where she was
and why. With fresh interest she examined her room,
hoping perhaps for some hints about its owner's person-
ality, and coming rapidly to the conclusion that he had
both exquisite taste and the money to indulge it. She was

no connoisseur of antique furniture, but she knew enough to recognise the chairs flanking the carved marble fireplace as Louis Quinze, and the charming figurines on the mantel were undoubtedly Sèvres porcelain. Embroidered brocade curtains fell in graceful folds to the floor, which was covered by an Aubusson carpet. Yet for all its richness, the room was meant to be lived in; there were a couple of books on the bedside table, and her own robe had been flung carelessly across one of the chairs.

A dainty ormolu clock chimed the hour: eleven o'clock. Amazed by how long she had slept, Andrea got up and dressed, and tiptoed down the staircase. At a loss, she hesitated, wondering which way to go. Claws rattling on the polished floor, two Samoyed huskies trotted in from a room to the right and stood regarding her with grave good manners.

She knelt, holding out her hand. 'Here, boys, come on.' As she had always had an empathy for animals, in no time one was allowing her to rub its head, while the other inquisitively sniffed the hem of her slacks. 'You're such beautiful creatures,' she crooned. 'What are your names?'

'The larger one is Oolik, and his sister is Sascha.'

Startled, Andrea turned on her heel, unaware of the charming picture she made kneeling on the sunlit floor beside the two furry white dogs. In the smooth fall of her hair, auburn lights gleamed against the creamy translucence of her skin; momentarily her thick lashes screened the warm brown of her eyes, so that they became as mysterious as a woodland pool. 'Oh, good morning,' she said, scrambling awkwardly to her feet. Her mouth quirked. 'Although it's almost good afternoon, isn't it?'

He surveyed her sombrely. Jolted in spite of herself by the smouldering grey of his eyes, she was forced to admit he was quite the most disturbingly handsome man she had ever seen. In the daylight she noticed how strongly hewn his tanned features were, and again discerned the hint of sensuousness in his mouth. But for all its strength and character, it was not a happy face; she longed to know what could have caused that almost excessive self-control and that underlying aura of bitterness.

His good looks were augmented by an intense masculinity as much a natural part of him as the ruffled black
hair and lean and rangy body. She wished he wasn't quite
so tall; it placed her at an immediate disadvantage, and for
a reason she did not analyse she did not wish to be at a
disadvantage with the formidable Mr Trent.

'Mrs Hamilton has breakfast ready for you in the dining
room,' he said briefly. 'Afterwards she'll show you to my
study.' On these rather ominous words he nodded to her,
called the dogs to heel and left her alone.

The condemned man—or woman—will now eat a hearty
meal, Andrea thought ruefully. And by chatting to the
housekeeper to keep her mind off the proposed interview,
she did manage to consume unladylike portions of crisp
bacon and eggs. Replete, she sat back. 'That was lovely,
Mrs Hamilton, thank you. You've been very kind,' she said.

The housekeeper smiled, pleased. She was short and
plump, her grey hair arranged in rigid waves and curls, and
appeared as friendly and approachable as her employer was
the reverse. 'It was a pleasure, dear. I like having a pretty
young thing like you around the house. And please call me
Maggie, everyone does.'

Andrea blushed at the compliment, looking doubly
pretty as she did so.

'Now come along,' Maggie continued, 'and I'll show you
where the study is. You needn't be anxious, he's only a
man, after all.'

Hiding a nervous sputter of laughter at this mundane
attitude, and wishing she could adopt it herself, Andrea
followed the older woman down the hall, its walls decorated with gold-framed floral prints. If she had felt awed by
the gleaming mahogany table and crystal chandeliers of the
dining room, she felt immediately at home in the study. A
peacock blue Persian rug lay on the smooth hardwood
floor, which reflected the play of flames from the granite
fireplace. A workmanlike oak desk, untidily heaped with
papers, dominated the furniture, but the comfortable armchairs, placed invitingly near the bookshelves, did not

escape her notice. And what bookshelves! Cynthia had more than once disparagingly labelled her niece a book-worm, but that had been the one criticism that could not bruise Andrea's feelings at all. In the bitter days after the accident the girl had found strength and solace in her books, and since then had never ceased to regard them as old friends. So it was to the neat ranks of multicoloured covers that her gaze flew, her fears temporarily forgotten. 'How lucky you are to have a room like this!' she exclaimed without a trace of envy, turning to him a piquant face alight with enthusiasm.

For a fleeting instant she was convinced that he shared her feelings, an instant that was heady with delight. But it was gone so quickly that afterwards she could not be sure if she had imagined it. 'Sit down, Miss MacKinlay,' he said formally, seating himself behind the barrier of the oak desk.

Ridiculously nervous, she folded her hands in her lap, and said with a composure she was far from feeling, 'I'm very grateful for your hospitality, Mr Trent. And I haven't thanked you adequately for coming to my rescue last night.'

'I'm still amazed that I didn't run you down,' he responded drily. 'One normally doesn't expect to discover young ladies in distress in the midst of a blizzard. If I may be allowed to ask, just where were you going?'

His sarcasm made her flinch. She hesitated, staring down at her interlocked fingers, knowing it would be impossible to tell this disturbing man the complete truth about yesterday's débâcle with Ronald Martin; the memory of it still made her shudder with shame. Nevertheless, as her host, he deserved some sort of an explanation. Because she was a truthful girl, she did not want to deliberately lie; she would have to omit large chunks of the story and hope for the best. Picking her words with care, she said, 'I've been employed at Stony Pass the last six months. Because of a misunderstanding, I resigned yesterday.'

She lifted her chin defiantly, daring him to ask what had happened. Although he must have sensed the gaps in her narrative, he remained silent, so she went on, 'I meant to catch the bus to Valleyfield, but I missed it.' His raised eyebrows caused her to add lamely, 'My watch had stopped.'

'Dear me, this is quite a comedy of errors, isn't it?' he said softly. 'Do go on.'

She flushed miserably and stumbled on. 'Well, rather than go back to Stony Pass, I decided to walk to Valleyfield and stay there overnight. I was sure I'd get a lift at least part of the way. I hadn't heard the weather forecast, you see.'

'Perhaps you'll make a practice of listening to it more often now,' was his unsympathetic comment. 'And where were you going once you'd reached Valleyfield? Is your home there?'

'Oh, no, my home is in Cape Breton.' She stopped abruptly, once again staring at her fingers. The old farmhouse had long since been sold, so why then did she persist in saying her home was there? She amended her statement, a thread of sadness in her voice, 'At least, it used to be there. No, I planned to catch the bus to Calgary and then the train to Halifax. My aunt has a house there.'

'That's a long way to go. Do you not have anyone closer than that?'

'No,' she replied unwillingly, resenting the inquisition but helpless to deflect it. 'My aunt is away, so the house is closed up, but she gave me a key in case I ever needed it.' And how angry she'll be to find me there when she gets back, Andrea thought unhappily, not realising how blatantly her telltale features revealed her emotions to the man watching her.

'Your parents? Or brothers and sisters?'

'My parents are dead and I was the only child.' Would his questions never end? Her knuckles whitened with the strain.

'No young man?'

'No.'

'I see. Well, Miss MacKinlay, since it appears no one is anxiously awaiting your arrival, I would suggest you stay here for the next couple of days. The roads are in an atrocious state today, and another ten inches of snow is predicted for tomorrow. Maggie is always glad to have guests, and since you're obviously a booklover, you shouldn't have any trouble keeping yourself amused.'

As though I was ten years old! she fumed inwardly, torn between gratitude for his offer and reluctance to be deeper in his debt. But overriding these emotions, her nerves tingled and throbbed with a primitive sense of danger. Her heartbeat quickened. Beware this man, something warned her. Escape while you still can, for if you don't, your life will never be the same again.

'That's very kind of you,' she said breathlessly, 'but I really can't impose on you any longer.'

'I assure you, you will not be imposing,' he said, an odd inflection in his voice.

She chose to ignore it. 'Thank you, Mr Trent, but I can't stay.'

'My dear girl, you have no choice,' was the lazy rejoinder, while his grey eyes mocked her temper-flushed cheeks. 'Please don't contemplate anything foolish like packing your suitcase and leaving by the back door, will you?' Her cheeks grew pinker, since that was exactly what she had been contemplating. Damn the man! He was a mind-reader as well as an autocrat.

'I can see you did have that plan in mind,' he continued with an insolent assurance she found infuriating. 'I won't allow it, you know.'

'What gave you the right to direct my life?' she exploded.

'If yesterday is any example, you don't seem particularly capable of directing it yourself.'

Unfortunately there was enough truth in his statement, that she was forced to subside. With a distinct effort of will she belatedly recalled her manners and was able to say coolly, 'In that case I must thank you again and accept your offer.'

'Excellent!' The mockery was open now. 'I'm glad you can accept the inevitable, it's a useful accomplishment.

Please make yourself at home, won't you? And now, if you
will excuse me, I really must get some work done.'

Unable to think of an adequate reply to this summary
dismissal, Andrea got up and left the room, shutting the
door behind her with exaggerated care. Not that the high
and mighty Stuart Trent would notice; he was already
engrossed in the papers on his desk. She let out her pent-
up breath in an angry sigh, glaring at the mirror on the
opposite wall as though it were her host she saw there and
not an image of herself, her cheekbones tinged with colour,
a wisp of dark hair across her forehead. She pushed it back
impatiently, feeling like a schoolgirl after a gruelling ses-
sion with the headmaster—or, more aptly, as though she
had been played with, as a cat plays with a mouse before
destroying it. She shuddered, again aware of an irrational
frisson of her nerves. What a metaphor to choose ... and
yet he possessed something of the powerful, dangerous
beauty of a mountain lion ...

Still smarting, she stalked down the corridor.

'There you are, dear,' said Maggie, and with characteris-
tic forthrightness added, 'Gracious, you do look cross! You
mustn't let his manner upset you, he's a grand man under-
neath. It takes a while to get to know him, that's all.'

I can believe it, Andrea thought irritably.

Head on one side, like an inquisitive bird, the housekeeper added, 'I do hope you're not going to rush off today,
are you, Miss MacKinlay?'

'I'm afraid not. I've been told in no uncertain terms to
stay for at least two more days. So that's that.'

'I'm very glad you are staying. This big house is so
isolated in the winter, and when Mr Stuart's working he
doesn't have much time for a chat.'

By now Andrea had calmed down enough to recognise
loneliness and the need for an audience in Mrs Hamilton's
chatter, and was ashamed for her own ungraciousness.
'What does he do?' she asked, glancing around at the
magnificently appointed lounge. 'Surely he doesn't have to
earn his living?'

'Oh, no, he's very well off. This house and the ranch

have been in the family for years. He writes plays, dear. Haven't you heard of Simon Ward?'

'Of course I have. Who hasn't?' She stared at the older woman. 'You don't mean Mr Trent is Simon Ward?'

Delighted by the effect she was causing, Maggie nodded in a conspiratorial fashion. 'Indeed I do.'

Andrea stood stock still, digesting this amazing information. She had read every one of his plays and attended performances of several. The most famous actors and actresses in the world clamoured for parts in a Simon Ward play, and it had long been one of her ambitions to attend a premiere performance on Broadway. Heavens, to think she had actually sat in his study!

'Usually he works on his plays through the winters,' Maggie explained. 'He likes to spend a lot of time on the ranch in summer. Of course, he has to make frequent trips to New York and Toronto and London. He's a very busy man.'

Andrea's thoughts about her host were now a mass of contradictions which she seemed unable to sort out, although somehow knowing who he was had eased some of the smart of his cross-examination. Trying not to think about him, she spent a pleasant afternoon with Maggie in the kitchen, making bread, preparing the evening meal, and chatting over domestic matters.

Because the housekeeper with innate tact asked no awkward questions, Andrea soon forgot to be shy, and by the end of the afternoon they considered each other as friends. 'Look at the time!' Maggie suddenly exclaimed in the middle of a discussion about jam-making. 'I had no idea it was so late. Hurry and get changed, dear, while I lay the table. Mr Stuart likes to eat promptly at seven.'

'Change? Whatever for?'

'Why, you're to have dinner with him, of course. Your slacks are very becoming, but possibly a dress or a skirt might be nicer? Mr Stuart never wears his work clothes for dinner.'

'Oh, dear,' Andrea wailed, 'I assumed I would be eating here with you.'

'No, no, he mentioned specially that you were to eat with him this evening.'

The prospect of a four-course meal alone with Stuart Trent in the vast elegance of the dining room was a daunting one, but it seemed that once again Andrea had no choice. She ran upstairs, taking the steps two at a time, then breathlessly surveyed the scanty contents of her wardrobe. If Maggie thought a dress would be 'nice', then a dress it would have to be; of the two she had with her, the light blue one was the more becoming. It was fashioned in a shirtwaist style, fitting her tiny waist snugly and flaring into a gored skirt, with a matching silk scarf tucked into the neckline. She made up her face with care, eye-shadow and mascara accentuating her long lashes, a tangerine lipstick outlining the innocent softness of her mouth. One eye on the clock drawing steadily nearer seven, she gathered her hair into a loose knot on top of her head, and put on her highest-heeled shoes—at least her arrogant host wouldn't tower over her quite so alarmingly. Delicate gold earrings and a spray of perfume and she was ready—only ten minutes late.

Leaving the room, she turned to close the bedroom door behind her, then jumped as a voice spoke from the shadows. 'How charming you look, Miss MacKinlay. Well worth waiting for!'

Heart fluttering against her ribs, Andrea stuttered, 'You frightened me. I didn't know you were there.'

'I'm sorry,' he drawled, his lazy grin belying his words. He moved closer to her, which did nothing to slow down her heartbeat. If she had thought him handsome in grey flannels and a thick sweater, he was now breathtaking in a superbly fitting camel-hair suit that subtly emphasised the breadth of his shoulders and narrowness of his hips. He moved, she thought, like a jungle animal, completely at home in his environment and completely confident of his prowess ... whereas she again felt like the hapless victim, mesmerised and helpless. She gave herself a mental shake, obscurely angry that he affected her so strongly, and said with the faintest hint of censure in her tone, 'Shall we go down? I'm afraid I'm a little late, but I hadn't realised I was to dine with you until Maggie told me.'

'Did I neglect to mention it this morning? Then it's my turn to apologise.' With a sardonic bow he offered her his arm, which after an instant's hesitation she took. As he glanced down at the slim ringless fingers gently resting on his sleeve, he brought up his other hand and with one long finger traced a blue vein across the back of her hand to her wrist. Some unknown emotion passed swiftly across his features and was gone, gone as quickly as it had come. Sensitive to every nuance of this man as she never had been to any other, Andrea knew she had not imagined it, yet it was beyond her ability to interpret it.

Stuart Trent looked up to find her face troubled, her eyes warm brown pools in the dusk. For a long moment their gazes locked in a wordless message that shook the girl to the depth of her being.

From downstairs the dinner bell rang, clear and prosaic. The strange mood of intimacy was shattered; they became again two strangers facing each other in a dimly lit hallway.

When the man spoke, Andrea was oddly disappointed that he sounded so calm and matter-of-fact. 'I asked Maggie to serve us in the sunroom, I thought you'd be more comfortable there. The dining room's fine for a formal dinner party, but I never eat there on my own. Come along.'

It was a delightful room decorated in gold and russet and green. Firelight sparkled on the crystal and silver arranged on a small oval table, while long velvet drapes shut out the winter night.

As though the fleeting interlude upstairs had been some sort of catharsis, Stuart Trent became a perfect host, skilfully guiding the conversation over topics as varied as wildlife conservation and Salvador Dali's painting, as well as providing Andrea with fascinating insights into some of the trials and tribulations of being a playwright. 'I'm in a real bind at the moment,' he commented, refilling her wine glass. 'The woman in Valleyfield who does all my typing has just had her second child, so it'll be at least two months before she can get back to work. By which time she'll be so far behind, I don't see how I'll make my dead-line at the publishers. I've scoured the entire valley from Indian Creek to the prairie for a typist, without any luck. I'll have to advertise, I suppose.'

Hardly daring to believe her ears and not giving herself time to think, Andrea volunteered, 'I can type.'

His knife clattered on his plate. 'You can? My dear girl, do you mean it?'

His careless endearment fell sweetly on her ears. Striv-ing to be practical, she said, 'Yes, I took a secretarial course two years ago. My speed might be a bit rusty, but I'm sure it would improve.'

'But that's splendid. You're a godsend.' He paused. 'I seem to be taking it for granted that you'll stay and work for me. Would you like time to consider?'

Andrea shook her head. It had been the easiest decision she had ever made and she could only marvel at her good fortune. 'No, I'd be very pleased to do your typing, and to help in any way I can.'

He raised his glass. 'A toast to my new assistant.' Andrea smiled, blushing with pleasure. 'To be practical for a minute,' he continued, 'we'll have to make arrangements about your salary. You can live here, which will work out very well. It was always a nuisance transporting tapes and rough drafts between here and Valleyfield. When would you like to start?'

'Tomorrow,' was the prompt reply.

When Maggie came in with dessert and coffee, she was told of the plan, and said comfortably, 'Everything always works out for the best, doesn't it?' She turned away so that neither Stuart nor Andrea saw the complacent quirk of her lips nor realised from her far-seeing eyes that she was busy building castles in the air.

Later, when Andrea finally reached the privacy of her room—and now it was truly her room—she went to the window, remembering in what a different mood she had stood at another window only yesterday. Now the frozen blackness held no threat for her, so unbelievably had her fortunes changed in the last twenty-four hours.

She smiled happily to herself. To think she had dreaded the tête-à-tête this evening with Stuart Trent, afraid it would be filled with long and awkward pauses. Instead he had been charming, treating her tentatively offered questions and comments with total seriousness, until, increasingly confidently, she had contributed her fair share of the conversation. It had been an intoxicating and unique experience; for years, by a deadly combination of sarcasm and derisive contempt, Cynthia had successfully discouraged her niece from self-expression, and most of Andrea's shyness could be traced back to her aunt's well-bred tinkle of laughter. Unworthily Andrea wished Cynthia could see her now—personal secretary to the famous Simon Ward—and then chided herself for being so petty. If she was going to be anyone's secretary, she'd better get to bed and have a good night's sleep.

CHAPTER TWO

Five minutes after Andrea entered Stuart Trent's study, the rosy glow of the evening before was dispelled with brutal speed. His brusque 'Good morning, Miss MacKinlay,' bore no relation to the warm 'Good night, Andrea,' of a few hours ago. With brisk efficiency he showed her the partially typed first act, the manuscript and the file of rough copy.

'I've set the other typewriter up in the sunroom for you, I think that will be a more convenient arrangement,' he said. 'Now listen closely. I have one unbreakable rule: if the study door is shut, it means I'm working, and you are not on any account to disturb me. If you have questions, they will just have to wait until I'm through. Is that clear?'

Andrea stammered, 'Yes, of course, Mr Trent,' thoroughly daunted by his dictatorial manner. She picked up the stack of papers and left the room, hearing the door click firmly behind her. So much for her airy daydreams of watching him at work, of being asked for help with a difficult passage, of chatting about the morning's progress over a cup of coffee. She was back to square one, the schoolgirl summarily dismissed from the headmaster's presence. Tears pricked her eyelids. Furiously blinking them away, she wondered how she could be so upset by a man she had not met two days ago.

She settled herself at the table in the sunroom, pushing away memories of last night's charming companion. Charm was the right word, she thought bitterly—charm that could be turned on and off at will, like a tap. Well, if he wanted to be cold and businesslike, then she would be the same. Grimly determined to be the best typist he had ever had, she set her mind to the task at hand.

Three hours later when Maggie brought lunch on a tray, it was an effort for Andrea to drag herself back to reality, so absorbed had she become in the story unfolding beneath her flashing fingers. She rubbed her eyes and stretched, suddenly aware that she was tired and aching in every limb, but in a glow of satisfaction noting the neat pile of completed sheets. She'd proofread them right after she'd eaten.

'Mr Stuart said you were to have a two-hour lunch break,' Maggie interjected. 'He suggested you might like to go outdoors.'

'Oh, did he?' Andrea sputtered indignantly. 'What happens if I don't want to? Besides, does he take a two-hour lunch break?'

'Now, dear, he only wants what's best for you. When he's in the middle of a play, it's rarely he takes a break at all. I have a hard time getting him to eat some days, it really worries me.'

'I don't think you need to worry about him,' Andrea retorted, in no mood to be overly sympathetic towards her exasperating employer. 'As it happens, I want to finish typing the first act and then go over what I've done so far. I may go out after that, I'll see.'

The housekeeper looked distressed. 'He's a hard man to cross,' she warned. 'Why don't you do as he suggests?'

'Nonsense!' Andrea said lightly. 'Mr Trent can run his own life as he likes, but he won't run mine as well. And now I must eat my lunch before it gets cold—it looks delicious.'

Within half an hour the tray had been pushed aside and the typewriter keys were clattering away merrily. Deaf to the opening door and to the fall of heavy footsteps across the carpet, Andrea gave a cry of alarm as the paper she was reading was jerked from under her nose. 'Did Maggie not tell you to rest for two hours?' Stuart Trent snapped.

In a glorious and unexpected sweep of emotion Andrea lost her temper for the second time in as many days. She sprang to her feet. 'Yes, Maggie did tell me to rest for two hours. But I told her, as I'm telling you now, that I prefer to keep on working. I am not a child, nor will I be treated like one!'

'You are behaving very much like a child, and a badly

spoiled one at that,' he grated, holding on to his own temper with an effort that clenched his hands by his sides and tightened his jaw. 'In fact, I feel like putting you across my knee and spanking you.'

'You wouldn't dare!'

'Don't bet on it.' He moved a step closer and grasped her by the shoulders, so near that she could see the angry pulse beating in his throat. 'Now just you listen to me, Miss Andrea MacKinlay. From now on you will work from nine to twelve and from two to four. Those are my orders and you will obey them, unconditionally. Do you understand, or do I have to turn you across my knee?' His fingers tightened cruelly on the soft flesh of her upper arms.

'You make yourself perfectly clear,' she answered coldly, only the faintest hint of a tremor in her voice. 'It's a pity you have to resort to brute strength to get your point across.'

For a moment she thought he was going to carry out his threat. He drew a long, harsh breath before deliberately releasing his hold. 'I'm sure I've never met a more exasperating female than you! Anyone else would be delighted to take two hours off; the problem nowadays is usually to get someone to do a decent day's work. You're different, I'll say that about you.'

'Thank you,' she said saucily.

'It's for your own good, you silly child. You're as pale as a ghost and as thin as a rake, if you'll pardon my hackneyed similes. You need to be out in the fresh air, and you need to put some flesh on your bones. I don't want to be accused of mistreating my secretary.' His anger had dissipated as quickly as it had come, and his mouth softened in a sudden disarming smile. 'And yes, I agree, I am dictatorial, autocratic, uncouth and bad-tempered. Nevertheless, you will do as I say, Andrea. Please?'

Her fury melted away under the warmth of his coaxing smile. She let out her breath in a tiny sigh of surrender. 'Very well.' With one last spurt of spirit she added. 'But you are dictatorial, you know.'

He grinned, running one hand through his already untidy hair, so that she longed to reach up and smooth it with her hand. 'Whatever you say, you little spitfire. The dogs would love to go for a walk, and Maggie will show you where the parkas and snowshoes are kept. Don't go too far, though, you can never trust the weather at this time of year. But I don't have to tell you that, do I?'

As she wrinkled her nose at him rudely, he laughed, turned on his heel and was gone. Feeling rather weak at the knees, Andrea sat down, her thoughts in utter confusion, only gradually coming to the realisation that she had been charmed by a man's smile into doing exactly as he wished. She should have added complex, confusing and contradictory to the list of adjectives describing Stuart Trent, she decided wryly. And now she'd better do as she was told.

Imperceptibly Andrea's days fell into a pattern which on the whole was productive and intensely satisfying. She thoroughly enjoyed typing the manuscript, taking pride in the quality of her work, and fascinated by the skilful development of character and suspense. Nor were her off-duty hours by any means tedious. She explored the environs of the house, coming to love the subdued glow of its bricks against the dazzling white snow, and the spiral of smoke ascending from the study chimney. Sturdy evergreen shrubs clustered round the patio, while the naked skeletons of oak and elm edged the driveway and the white-fenced paddock.

The spacious shingled stables, filled with the scent of last summer's hay, sheltered only two horses, a chestnut stallion named Shah, and a much smaller Arabian mare, Star of the East. Although a little afraid of the stallion, Andrea impartially distributed carrots to both horses, afterwards lingering to stroke the mare's smooth neck and talk nonsense into her pricked ears. There was a family of newborn kittens in the hay, and high in the gloomy cobwebbed rafters pigeons cooed away the winter days. It was for Andrea a place where she could recapture happy memories of her parents' farm, and where some of the troubles of the intervening years could be forgotten.

The ranch proper was almost a mile away from the house, a good distance for snowshoeing. It consisted of a neat array of barns, machine sheds and bunkhouses, now occupied by only a small crew of men, since even in winter the cattle were out on the range.

Almost daily Andrea would don the snowshoes, glad that her knee was giving her no further trouble. On fine days she and the two huskies travelled along the forest trails, which were tracked by deer and moose and inhabited by flocks of chickadees and redpolls. Although she hated to admit it, Stuart Trent had been right—she had needed more exercise to bring colour back to her cheeks and a new spring to her step. Maggie's excellent cooking was remedying the other fault he had found in her: 'thin as a rake' still rankled.

Considering their working relationship she saw very little of her employer, and when she did see him he was usually preoccupied and taciturn to the point of rudeness. Their intimate dinner of the first evening was never repeated, and indeed she sometimes wondered if she had dreamed it, embarrassed to recall how eagerly she had responded to him. She was even more ashamed to find herself looking and hoping for a quick smile or a word of praise from him, only to be disappointed time and time again. He scarcely seemed to know she existed, she mused, piqued in a very feminine way that this should be so.

He himself was the one who finally gave her the reason for his withdrawn and brooding silences, a reason that gentled Andrea's resentment and transformed it into a compassion that, had she but known it, was infinitely more dangerous . . .

It was about a fortnight after she arrived. As usual she went to his study first thing in the morning to get her work for the day. He was already seated at his desk. 'I'll be with you in a moment,' he said irritably, scarcely raising his eyes from the page.

Andrea studied his face with secret concern, for he did not appear to have slept at all last night. However, she no longer expected him to confide any of his personal affairs in her, so she wandered over to the bookshelves and began idly thumbing through some paperbacks. A gold-framed photograph, that had been displaced by an untidy pile of books, caught her eye; she dusted it off and examined it with interest. Two small children grinned out at her. They were perhaps six or seven years old, clad identically in T-shirts and shorts, each with a mop of curly black hair, cropped short on the boy, tumbling on the shoulders of the girl. They bore a startling resemblance to Stuart Trent, their sunny smiles catching at her heart. Could it be a picture of him as a child? He had never mentioned a sister.

'I'm ready, Andrea, whenever you are.' His words had their usual edge of sarcasm.

For once not paying it any heed, she held out the photograph and said impulsively, 'What delightful children!'

He got up from the desk and took the frame from her hand, staring at the two happy little faces as though he had never seen them before. 'That must have been taken a couple of years ago.'

'Oh,' she said blankly. 'I had assumed the boy was you.'

He frowned at her. 'Me? Of course not. They're my children.'

Stunned, Andrea repeated, 'Your children? But you told me you weren't married!'

'My wife died four years ago,' he said in a tone that brooked no further questions on the subject. Andrea waited with bated breath. 'The twins are eight now. They go to school in Calgary, that's why you haven't seen them yet. They'll be home for their Easter holidays in a few days.'

'Don't you miss them?' she blurted, her innate tact vanishing from the shock of his disclosures.

He flinched as if she had struck him. She longed to snatch back her hasty question, but it was too late, the unkind words were already spoken. 'Of course I do,' he answered roughly. 'But how could I keep them here? Mrs Hamilton is too old to have charge of them, and as for me, when I'm not writing, I'm away, or at the ranch. They get much more attention at school than they would here.'

Andrea was horrified to hear her unruly tongue say, 'Perhaps not the right kind, though.' Stubbornly she continued, 'You're their father, and home is where they belong.'

He rubbed his forehead with unsteady fingers. 'What kind of a home is it without a mother?' he demanded. 'After Barbara, I could never marry again. No, they're better off where they are.'

Distressed out of all proportion, Andrea wished the conversation had never started, and strove to find a way to end it gracefully, without further lacerating his feelings. 'They're beautiful children, and you must be very proud of them,' she said finally. 'I'll look forward to meeting them. Tell me, what are their names?'

'Heather and Bruce.' A reluctant grin made Stuart Trent look ten years younger. 'I guess I'm looking forward to seeing them too. They always manage to turn the entire house upside down in the first five minutes they're here, the little monkeys. It always seems so quiet ... and empty after they're gone.'

'I'll have to show them the kittens in the barn,' Andrea offered, wanting to keep his smile in place.

His eyes, serious and strangely vulnerable, met her candid brown ones, and she knew he had guessed her purpose. 'I hope you will do that, Andrea. By the way, did anyone ever tell you you're a good listener?'

She lowered her thick lashes, confused and pleased by his compliment. 'I don't think so,' she murmured.

'Well, you are. It's a rare gift.' He glanced again at the photograph. 'I must keep this on my desk, I don't want to lose it again. And talking about desks, we'd better tackle the second act. I wrote a fresh draft last night, I wasn't satisfied with the previous one.'

The intimacy between them, all too brief, was over. When Andrea went to the sunroom, she found it difficult to concentrate on the task at hand. So Stuart Trent was a widower, and had been for four long years. It was painfully obvious he could neither forget his wife, nor bear the thought of replacing her—how he must have loved her!

The harsh lines in his face, the unhappiness in those grey eyes, were now explained. She wished there were some way she could help him, although she did not see how, unless she could spend some of her spare time with his children and ensure they enjoyed their few days at home. Having resolved to do this, she immediately felt better. Furthermore, she had convinced herself that now she knew the reason behind Stuart Trent's moodiness, she would be able to cope with, or even avert, the frequent clashes that seemed to flare up between them—she would be patient and understanding.

Like so many good resolutions, Andrea's was short-lived. That very afternoon, her employer strode into the sunroom and said curtly, 'Leave that for now. I have a couple of things to do in Valleyfield and you can come with me.'

As usual he managed to arouse in her a mixture of conflicting emotions. She was both surprised and pleased by the proposed change in routine, yet also was annoyed to have the invitation phrased more as an order than as a request. She stared at him, not realising how clearly her dilemma was expressed in her mutinous brown eyes.

'What's wrong?' he asked.

'It's customary to ask if I'd like to go, not to tell me I'm going.'

He ran his fingers through his hair impatiently, the familiar glint of anger in his eyes. 'You're a touchy little thing, aren't you?' he exclaimed, and without waiting for an answer, added, 'Look, it's the end of the month, so I must give you your pay-cheque. You can cash it in Valleyfield if you want to. Are you coming or not?'

'Yes!' she snapped.

'Get your jacket. I'll wait for you outside.'

So much for patience and understanding, thought Andrea ruefully, as she hurriedly pulled on her green parka and hunted for her mittens . . . she wouldn't put it past him to go without her if she kept him waiting too long. However, when she raced downstairs, he was standing by the jeep, rugged and broad-shouldered in the same sheepskin jacket he had been wearing the first time she saw him. His glance swept over her in casual appraisal; he was as aloof and unapproachable as the distant mountains, and somehow equally dangerous. For in the privacy of her thoughts Andrea was honest enough to acknowledge how strongly he always affected her. Anger, fear, trust, compassion: he had aroused them all in her—in fact, everything but indifference.

'Shall we go?' he said with exaggerated forbearance. 'Or shall we stand here staring at each other all afternoon?'

She glowered at him. 'I'm ready when you are, Mr Trent.'

'The name is Stuart,' he grated, 'or haven't you noticed I've been calling you by your first name all week?'

Of course she had noticed, but she couldn't admit that to him, so she contented herself with climbing into the jeep in a studious silence.

As they drove away, he dug his hand in his pocket and passed her a plain brown envelope. 'Your cheque.'

'Thank you,' she responded politely, and slit it open; the amount was more than twice her salary at the Martins'. 'But that's far too much!'

'Andrea,' he said, with an edge of steel in his voice, 'you and I manage to argue about everything else under the sun. We will not argue about your salary.'

'Very well,' she answered meekly, already knowing better than to differ with him when he used that tone. Delightedly she began doing mental arithmetic; she could send Cynthia double the amount she had been sending her previously, which meant she could pay back the rest of that hated debt—she ticked it off in her mind—six months. Only six months! And then she would be free of her obligation to Cynthia, free to go where she pleased and do as she liked. Wholly occupied by these pleasant reflections, she paid scant attention to her escort, and as they drove down the main street of Valleyfield her eyes were already searching for the bank.

'I'll drop you off here,' Stuart said. 'Why don't we meet at the hotel restaurant in an hour? Will that be long enough for you?'

Andrea nodded eagerly. 'That's plenty of time, thanks.'

Her face broke into a charming smile and impulsively she touched his sleeve. 'I'll see you later.' She knew he didn't understand her happiness—how could he?—but she had wanted to share it.

Her business took considerably less than an hour; she cashed the cheque, composed a carefully noncommittal letter to Cynthia, and enclosed a money order. Then, with free time but very little money on her hands, she wandered down the bustling little street. The air was milder today with a hint of spring in it. The sidewalks were thronged with gaily dressed skiers from the nearby slopes, with cowboys in dungarees and stetsons, with housewives and children. After she had bought a couple of pocketbooks in a drugstore, Andrea's attention was caught by a small dress shop tucked between the library and the post office, and she gazed raptly at the single garment displayed in the window. It was a dinner dress of silk jersey, the rose-coloured material falling in soft folds from a high waist to the floor. Instinctively she knew it would suit her; how she wished she could buy it! It was impossible, of course. After deducting Cynthia's money, there was hardly any left, and just as she was sure the dress would fit, she was equally sure it would be expensive, it was that sort of shop. Anyway, where would she have the opportunity to wear such a dress? She sighed, her lips drooping unconsciously.

'Buy it,' said a familiar voice in her ear, 'and I'll take you out for dinner in Calgary next week.'

She looked up, already knowing who it was; for once, Stuart's grey eyes were oddly gentle. 'I wish I could,' she replied wistfully, 'it's so beautiful.'

'Go ahead,' he coaxed. 'The colour would become you.'

'I can't afford it,' she said baldly, storing away the implied compliment for later consideration.

He looked at the small package of books in her hand, a puzzled frown on his forehead. 'My dear girl, you surely haven't spent all of that cheque already?'

A guilty flush stained her cheeks, while she hung her head, momentarily speechless. She hated to be dishonest and evasive with him of all people, but to tell him the truth was impossible. To explain the debt to her aunt would entail the whole unhappy story of the accident, which in turn would lead inevitably to the preceding months of glorious achievement. Her face tightened. She had blocked those exhilarating days so completely from her memory that she could not even think about them herself, let alone reveal them to the enigmatic man at her side.

She took refuge in anger, her voice sharp. 'Surely how I spend my money is my own affair. I'm only your secretary, after all, not your wife!' She bit her lips, appalled by her runaway tongue, but the damage was done.

'It's hard to understand how you can look so honest and be so deceitful,' he said savagely. 'Don't worry, Andrea, I won't enquire into your private life again. But you must admit it's rather full of interesting gaps, isn't it? This job you had in Stony Pass that terminated so mysteriously— what happened there? And the way you'll chatter on about your old home in Cape Breton, but never mention the years after that . . . I thought I could trust those big brown eyes of yours, but it seems I was wrong.'

Each word fell like a stone on her heart. A film of tears blurred her vision and only stubborn pride prevented them from spilling down her white cheeks.

'And for God's sake, don't start to cry. That's the oldest trick in the book,' he said roughly. 'I've done the errands I had to do here, and as you seem to have gone through all your money, I suggest we head back and forget about the restaurant. Strangely enough, I'm not hungry.'

The fifteen-minute drive back to the ranch was accomplished in hostile silence. The jeep pulled to a stop by the front door and Andrea got out, trembling in evey limb. Not waiting for Stuart Trent, she fled to her room, slammed the door, and fell on the bed in a storm of weeping, his bitter words echoing in her mind. Finally she dropped off into an exhausted slumber.

The next few days were mercifully busy ones. Stuart had finished the final draft of the play, and Andrea typed and retyped, striving to produce a perfect copy; at least she would not give him cause to complain that she was a less than competent secretary, whatever he might think of her morals. All week he did not address one sentence to her that was not concerned with business, and indeed went out. of his way to see as little of her as possible. Why this should hurt Andrea as much as it did, she was afraid to wonder. To add to her misery, she could not help remembering his invitation in front of the dress shop ... dinner in Calgary ... the two of them entering an elegant dining room, she wearing the long silk dress ... she gave herself a mental shake, banishing the bittersweet fantasy; he couldn't even speak a civil word to her, let alone have any further desire for her company.

Andrea continued in this frame of mind until one morning early in April, when Maggie blithely dropped a bombshell. 'I'm so looking forward to seeing my sister tomorrow, dear,' she said comfortably. 'She lives in British Columbia, and I haven't seen her since Christmas. I go there every Easter while Mr Stuart has the children home. I expect you're excited about going to Calgary with him, aren't you? Have you been there before?'

For a minute Andrea wondered if the housekeeper was playing a particularly cruel joke on her. 'Whatever do you mean?' she said slowly. 'I'm not going to Calgary.'

'Isn't he a dreadful man!' Maggie clucked. 'So forgetful. Two weeks ago, when I asked for the time off, it was arranged that both of you would go to the city to get Heather and Bruce. You couldn't stay here alone, dear. And now he hasn't remembered to tell you about it. I'll remind him first thing this morning. His head's in the clouds when he's in the middle of one of his plays ... I wouldn't put it past him to forget the children!'

'Please don't remind him about taking me,' Andrea begged. 'I'd be fine on my own, because I'm not frightened of being alone ...' Not nearly as frightened as I am of being with him, she thought. 'I really don't want to go to Calgary.'

The housekeeper looked nonplussed, perhaps sensing undercurrents, yet not wanting to pry. 'Many's the girl would jump at the chance of a trip with the famous Simon

Ward, you know,' she chided. 'I'm sure you'd have a nice time if you went.'

As a result of this conversation, Andrea was at least partly prepared for Stuart Trent's opening gambit later that morning. 'I guess Maggie mentioned the visit to Calgary, didn't she? We'll be leaving tomorrow afternoon and returning with the children the following evening.'

'I'd rather not go,' Andrea said stiffly, bracing herself for battle. 'I'll be quite all right here. You won't be gone that long.'

'Don't be silly, of course you can't stay alone—this place is much too isolated. What would you do if a blizzard came up like the one you arrived in? Just because it's April it doesn't mean winter's necessarily over.'

'I'm sure I'd survive.'

'Well, you're not going to have the chance to prove it,' he said flatly. 'And I presume you're not so selfish that you want Maggie to cancel her plans just so you can stay home?'

Cut to the quick, Andrea flared, 'You really don't think much of me, do you?'

'You're an excellent secretary, and that's all that concerns me,' was the cool reply. 'But as we're planning to spend the best part of two days together, let's endeavour to be civil to each other, shall we? I certainly don't want the children upset by any of your temper tantrums.'

'I shall be a model of decorum,' Andrea promised, the words belied by her flashing brown eyes.

Incredibly, he laughed. 'You'll have to do better than that if you're going to look the part.' He paused, one eyebrow raised sardonically. 'As I recall, I invited you for dinner, didn't I? The invitation still stands, Andrea. Be ready to leave mid-afternoon.' On this final command he left the room, leaving her as usual a prey to various emotions. Temper tantrums, indeed! But beneath her indignation, there spread a treacherous glow of anticipation; her fantasy was apparently to be realised after all.

The next day Maggie caught the westbound bus after lunch, and Andrea hurried upstairs to finish packing. Not that it would take long, she thought with regret, wishing she had something new and different to wear. But when she had showered, and brushed her long hair until it shone, and dressed in her slim-fitting blue jumpsuit, she could not help feeling pleased with her reflection in the full-length mirror.

A knock came at the door. 'Ready, Andrea?'

She opened it and smiled shyly at Stuart. 'Almost.'

He picked up her coat from the bed and held it out for her, his hands brushing her shoulders. Aware of his closeness in every nerve of her body, she bent to pick up her case; he reached for it simultaneously, and his hand fell warm on hers. Thoroughly confused, she dropped the handle as though it had stung her and the top of her head bumped his chin. Quickly his other arm encircled her waist to steady her.

'I—I'm sorry,' she stammered. 'Did I hurt you?'

She raised her eyes to meet his. As had happened once before, for a few intense seconds she experienced with him a strange sense of communication that was wordless and timeless . . . and perfect. Then, still holding her suitcase, he straightened and released her, breaking the fragile web that bound them. 'No,' he said quietly, 'you didn't hurt me. Shall we go?'

It was a beautiful afternoon, the sun bright in the clear blue sky, the snow-capped mountains glaring white. The road wound through the rolling foothills, where the snow lay deep in the hollows, although the open ground was now bare and brown.

'Stuart, look!' Andrea cried suddenly. 'They're moose, aren't they?'

'Mmmm, that's right,' he agreed, adding indulgently, 'Want me to stop the car?'

'Please.' She opened the door as quietly as she could and stepped out on to the shoulder of the road, where Stuart joined her, paying her, had she but guessed it, more attention than the grazing animals. The great bull moose raised his head, his spread of antlers held high. Then hunger overcoming caution, he resumed browsing on the low shrubs.

'They've done well to survive,' Stuart said. 'It's been a long hard winter, with exceptionally heavy snowfalls. Let's hope this is the final straw. The cow should drop her calf in a couple of weeks. You won't see her so close to the road then.'

Entranced, Andrea said warmly, 'Thanks for stopping, Stuart.'

'So you do know my name,' he said quizzically.

She blushed, only then realising how easily his name had slipped from her tongue. 'I'm on my best behaviour, hadn't you noticed?' she retorted, her pert reply an attempt to cover her discomfiture. She tried to recover the thread of the conversation. 'Moose are rare back East, so it's a treat for me to see them.'

'Well then, it's been my pleasure,' he said quietly.

She smiled, reassured by his obvious sincerity. They returned to the car; the constraint between them seemed to have vanished and in a relaxed, companionable silence they continued their journey. In front of them stretched the endless prairie, over a thousand miles of grassy plains spanning three provinces. The horizon was spiked with Calgary's skyscrapers, that grew ever closer as Stuart's Mercedes smoothly ate up the miles. Before they knew it, the city had engulfed them with its traffic, buildings, crowds, and ceaseless noise . . . another world, as different from the secluded peace of the ranch as night from day.

'We'll check in at the hotel first,' said Stuart, skilfully weaving in and out of the lines of cars and eventually pulling up in front of an old fashioned grey-stone façade in an expensive quarter of the city. He stopped the car. The liveried doorman came down the steps, the sun gleaming on his gold epaulettes.

'Let me help you, madam. Good afternoon, Mr Trent. Good to see you again. I hope you've been well?'

'Thanks, Henderson. How's the family these days?'

'Just fine, sir. The bellboy will look after your luggage

and I'll see that your car is parked for you. This way, madam.'

He led them into the lobby. Andrea was awed by the vast hallway, its vaulted ceilings scrolled in gilt, and its walls panelled in dark oak. Ornately carved furniture flanked a massive stone fireplace over which hung an oil painting of some long-ago battle. The thickly carpeted floor muffled the sounds of their footsteps as they approached the desk.

'I believe you have reservations for two rooms,' said Stuart, obviously unaffected by all this magnificence.

'Certainly Mr Trent. Rooms 908 and 910. Thomas will show you up.'

Andrea's room, which had its own fireplace, exuded the same luxury.

'This place is a bit of a museum piece,' Stuart remarked, 'but the service is excellent. I can't stand these modern chrome and plastic boxes that they call hotels nowadays!'

He tipped the bellboy and they were left alone. Putting a casual arm around her shoulders, he led her to the window. Dusk was falling over the city, its high buildings silhouetted against the clear golden sky. He pointed to a needle-like structure that rose thin and tall above the rectangular skyscrapers.

'There's the Calgary Tower. We'll have dinner there tonight. I think you'll enjoy that.'

'You're looking after me very well,' she said softly, feeling secure and yet excited by the protective circling of his arm.

He turned slightly and lowered his head, so close that she could see the pulse beating in his throat. His lips met hers in a gentle, searching kiss. She became intensely aware of the warmth and the strength of his body pressed against hers.

Slowly he moved back, his eyes dark in the gathering dusk. For a moment she thought he was about to speak; but destroying their moment of closeness the sharp insistent ring of the telephone sounded in his room. Stuart muttered an expletive under his breath. 'I'd better answer it, I suppose.' He turned and strode through the door that adjoined their rooms.

Dreamily leaning against the windowsill, Andrea gazed across the darkening city, listening to the steady rhythm of Stuart's voice in the next room with only half her mind. In a glow of wonder and delight she thought, he kissed me ... Stuart kissed me ... how remote their quarrels seemed in this newly discovered intimacy! How different was the sureness and respect of Stuart's touch from Ronald's drunken ardour!

The click of the phone in the next room indicated that his conversation had ended. Mildly curious, she called, 'Is everything all right?'

He rejoined her by the window. 'Yes, it was the school. Apparently there's to be a skating party tomorrow morning at the school rink before the children leave for their holidays. We'll have to rent ourselves some skates. We can do that first thing in the morning, though.'

Her heart began to thud. Trying very hard to sound normal, she said, 'But I ... can't skate.'

'You mean you've never learned? Don't they have rinks in the Maritimes?' he questioned jokingly.

'Of course they do,' she snapped. 'I just ... can't, that's all.'

Totally insensitive to the tremor in her voice, he said, 'Nonsense, anyone can learn to skate, if they want to.'

'Well, I don't want to! And I'm not going to! I'll go shopping in the morning instead.'

'You can't, you haven't any money, remember?' he said with controlled anger. 'The least you can do is come and watch.'

Andrea knew this was impossible. She had not been near a rink in two years. The bitter memories came crowding in and she cried, 'No! I won't come!'

He made one last effort to control his temper. 'Andrea, it's not much that I'm asking you to do.'

If only he knew that he was asking her to do the most difficult thing in the world, she thought desperately. Feeling trapped, she heard her voice, hollow and shaken, reiterate, 'No, I can't.'

Unmasked fury flared in his eyes, then he turned from her abruptly. 'Wait here!'

She watched in stricken silence as he went to his room and returned, flinging a flat cardboard box upon her bed.

'I have some business to attend to. I'll pick you up at eight.'

The door slammed shut behind him.

Her fingers fumbling with the cord, she lifted the lid of the box. Carefully wrapped in tissue was the silk dinner dress she had seen in Valleyfield. Pain, knife-sharp, constricted her throat. Tears ran slowly down her cheeks. She stroked the silken fabric, while her bewildered mind groped with the implications of this unexpected gift. Why had he done this? Try as she might, she could not understand his reasoning. All she knew was that she would have to wear it tonight, and somehow face his scornful eyes and his bitter enmity. She couldn't do it, she thought, she simply couldn't . . .

CHAPTER THREE

FAR below them the lights of Calgary, diamond-bright, twinkled in the blackness. For a moment the fascinating sight made Andrea forget her unhappiness.

'The tower is revolving very slowly,' Stuart said, his voice impersonal. 'We're over six hundred feet up, so it's quite a view, isn't it? In the daytime you can see the Rockies, they're only eighty miles to the west.'

Dressed in a dark business suit, he was seated across from her, his face tired and lined. She did not realise how shadowed and tense were her own features, nor how the deep rose shade of her dress failed to pick up any matching colour in her cheeks. The dress had fitted her perfectly, as she had known it would, its long skirt falling gracefully about her feet, its deep V-neckline partially exposing the creamy skin of her firm young breasts. She had needed every scrap of the self-assurance the dress had given her to meet Stuart again, to drive with him across the city and to endure the pain of their laboured dialogue. The food, beautifully prepared as it was, was tasteless in her mouth; she only wanted the evening to end so she could escape to her room and lock the door behind her. Somehow she had to prepare herself for the further ordeal of tomorrow morning.

It was almost a relief when another couple, friends of Stuart's, stopped by the table and Stuart invited them to join himself and Andrea. The conversation became general, and sooner than she had hoped, the meal was over. In silence again she and her escort drove back to their hotel.

In the lobby he took her firmly by the arm, his fingers digging into her bare flesh.

'Come on, I need a drink. Then you can go to your room as you've been wanting to do for the last two hours.'

She flushed painfully, for she had hoped she had been

48

able to disguise her desperate weariness and longing for privacy. The bar was decorated in the style of an old English pub and was almost deserted. She sank down into one of the deep armchairs, sipping slowly at the drink Stuart had ordered for her. Not wanting to talk to him, or even to look at him, she let her eyes wander around the room, abstractedly admiring the heavy carved beams in the ceiling, and the arrangement of horse brasses on the firescreen. Although the television above the bar was turned on, she paid it scant attention, its screen a mere blur of colour.

After the distressing quarrel of the afternoon and the constrained dinner she and Stuart had shared, she had at last reached a plateau of floating detachment where nothing seemed to matter very much. Perhaps it was the effect of the drink, for they had already had wine with their meal.

It was the music that brought her back to the present, that and the television announcer's voice . . .

'We have just seen the winning performance in the Senior Women's Division of the Canadian Figure Skating Championships in Toronto. This championship has been marred by an injury to one member of the Ontario team, who suffered a severe fall yesterday during her compulsory free-skating. Such accidents happen more frequently than the public realises. Last year two girls were unable to compete owing to last-minute injuries, and the year before, of course, we all remember how Andrea MacKinlay, who was favoured to win the gold medal, so badly damaged the cartilage of her knee that she was forced to retire completely from competitive skating. Here is a flashback to her winning performance in Ottawa . . .'

The music started. The familiar lilt of a Liszt rhapsody carried Andrea back into the past; unconsciously she leaned forward, her hands gripping the edge of the table, her eyes focused on the screen with painful intensity. In the spotlight the slim brown-haired figure swooped and leaped and glided on the shining surface of the ice. The skater was at one with the music, every moment a study of perfect grace and control. Spreadeagle, Arabian cartwheel, double toe-loop, sit spin . . .

Abruptly the announcer's face returned to the screen. Just as abruptly Andrea was jolted back to the present, to an awareness of her white-knuckled grip on the table, and to an awareness of the shocked comprehension in Stuart's eyes. His hand reached for hers, but blindly she pushed it aside. Her wrist struck the glass, which fell to the floor, where it shattered as quickly and completely as her own life had been shattered two years before.

In one lithe movement she pushed back her chair, knowing only that she must flee . . . across the room . . . through the lobby . . . into the confinement of the elevator.

In her room she flung herself on the bed in a storm of weeping. No longer could she contain her emotions as the memories crowded back—the hours of solitary practice, the nervousness before a competition, the exhilaration of a perfect performance, the excitement of applause—and all of this had been lost in one brief miscalculation, one wrong move.

She became aware of an almost imperceptible movement beside the bed. It was Stuart.

'Oh, please,' she pleaded, 'go away and leave me alone.'

But he did not go away. Instead she felt him sit beside her on the bed. A strong hand gently touched her shoulder.

'Andrea, Andrea, why didn't you tell me?'

'It's over. It's all finished. I couldn't bear to talk about it,' she sobbed.

She felt him gather her into his embrace, lifting her until her face was buried in his shirt-front. She was crying in earnest now, her tears soaking into his shirt. She could feel the slow steady beat of his heart against her cheek; it was inexpressibly comforting. Slowly she grew calmer, although her breath still came in ragged sighs. He held her close, rocking her gently in his arms, one hand stroking the silken thickness of her hair.

'Oh, Andrea, I'm so sorry. I wish you'd told me.'

Her fists clenched, she pounded ineffectively against the muscled hardness of his body.

'Don't pity me! I don't want anyone's pity!'

He reached into his pocket and pulled out a clean white handkerchief. 'Here, blow,' he said, with male practicality. She did as she was told, and finally raised her tear-streaked face to look at him.

'I got your shirt all wet,' she quavered.

'It'll dry. Don't worry about it.' He paused thoughtfully. 'And as for pity, you have to understand there's a great difference between pity and what I'm feeling now. Damn it, I don't pity you! Of course I'm sorry that a tragic accident robbed you of something you'd worked so hard for—I'd have to be totally insensitive not to feel that. But don't confuse it with pity.'

'I'm not sure I see the difference,' she murmured, shifting a little to rest more comfortably in his arms, and straining to fathom his expression in the darkness.

He pushed a strand of hair back from her forehead, frowning in concentration as he carefully chose his words.

'I don't know whether I can explain it, but I'll try. I would pity something or someone too weak to help himself. But you're young and beautiful and alive, and you still have so much to live for.'

He was rubbing his cheek against her hair. Warmth stole back into her limbs. Completely relaxed, she let her whole weight lean on his masculine strength.

'I think I understand what you mean.'

'Good. Now comes the sermon. You've obviously avoided coming to terms with your loss, Andrea. You haven't put on a pair of skates since it happened, have you?'

'No. How could I?'

'That's silly. Just because you can't do a triple jump—does this mean you can never enjoy skating again?'

'Well . . . I suppose not.'

'Of course not. There's more to skating than competition. Nevertheless, you do have to realise that that part of your life is over, and go on to something else. But don't just bury something that was of so much importance to you . . . There, that's all I have to say—end of sermon!'

Groping with these ideas, that were quite new to her,

Andrea said with heartfelt sincerity, 'I wish you'd been around two years ago. There was no one I could talk to who understood. I don't think I've ever felt so unhappy and so lonely in my life.'

'What about your aunt? Where was she?'

Andrea shuddered, burrowing deeper into the protective warmth of his arms.

'She was part of the problem—oh dear, it's all so complicated! You see, when my parents died, my father left money for my training, but it wasn't enough. So after it was gone, Aunt Cynthia loaned me some; she expected me to turn professional, I guess, and to be able to repay her in no time. After the accident she made it quite clear that I was to repay her anyway. Where do you think my first pay-cheque went?'

'Doesn't she have any money of her own?'

'Goodness, yes. But she says a debt is a debt.' Andrea added wryly, 'Knowing Cynthia, I guess I'm lucky she's not charging me interest!'

'So that's where your money went. No wonder you evaded all my questions.' His arms tightened in a sudden bear hug. 'My dear girl, how much simpler the truth would have been!'

'I can see that now,' she said defensively. 'But it's always easier to say what one should have done after the fact.'

'Of all people I can vouch for that,' he responded bitterly, a quick look of pain flashing in his dark eyes.

'What do you mean?' she questioned, surprised by this turn in their conversation.

His face became a mask of inscrutable emotions that Andrea could not comprehend. He said with difficulty, 'I once did something I shouldn't have done—and I paid for it for years.'

'What happened, Stuart?'

She felt his body tense with resistance, as he gave a harsh sigh. 'A marriage that should never have taken place . . . the cost was much too great.'

It was obvious to Andrea that Stuart had loved his wife

dearly and as a result of his loss, would probably never remarry. With his arms still holding her protectively, this knowledge seemed incredibly hard to bear.

Abruptly conscious of her cramped limbs, she moved slightly, not wanting to disturb their closeness. His lips moved from her hair and sought her mouth. A flame of joy was lit within her as his mouth moved against hers, first gently and then with increasing passion. She felt herself fall back against the pillow, his big body crushing her into the bed. His kiss became insistent, while of their own volition her fingers moved to caress his neck, one hand burying itself in his thick hair. Her body was being consumed by feelings that were totally new to her, so that, suddenly frightened, she wrenched her mouth from his.

His breathing was harsh in the darkness. 'You're so beautiful, Andrea,' he groaned. 'I didn't mean to frighten you.' His hands slid to her waist and with latent strength he quickly pulled her to her feet.

Needing his support, for she was trembling in every limb, she rested her head against his chest. She felt his strong hands firmly push her from him.

'I never want to hurt you, Andrea,' he murmured, 'but as I'm only human, I'm going to leave you now. Good night, my dear, sleep well,' and he was gone.

Andrea sank back on to the bed, her blood singing in her veins. How tender his voice had been when he had bade her goodnight! As she remembered his touch her body shivered with delight. What was happening to her? How could this man whom she had known for so short a time affect her so deeply? Love ... she had never loved a man before. How could love have grown from the stormy relationship between her and Stuart? Was it love? And what of Barbara, the wife whose loss he still mourned? She had left wounds that had not healed; deeply scarred as he was, could he ever love another woman?

Too tired to dwell any longer on these new conflicts, she slipped out of her dress and hung it carefully in the cupboard. Her first gift from him ... would it be the last?

It was morning. Andrea had slept deeply and dreamlessly

and woke now to bright rays of early morning sunlight falling across her bed. She stretched luxuriously and experienced a feeling of physical and emotional comfort. Full of anticipation for the day ahead she leaped out of bed and pulled open the curtain, a beatific smile on her face. It was going to be a beautiful day!

Just as she finished dressing a knock came at the door. 'Come in!' she called.

'Good morning, Andrea,' Stuart said. A wave of shyness swept over her. He was wearing an ivory Aran knit sweater over dark brown whipcord trousers, the former in startling contrast to his thick black hair. He smiled at her and all she could think of was the warmth and tenderness of his lips against hers such a brief time ago. He was so incredibly handsome! Indolently he leaned his tall body against the doorframe, while his eyes surveyed her from head to foot.

'You're looking lovely this morning,' he drawled, appreciatively eyeing her pink cheeks. She was wearing tailored slacks with a bulky knit grey and white sweater, her hair tumbling in silken waves over the collar.

He grinned with open friendliness. 'Don't be shy with me, Andrea. Let's go and eat, I'm starving!'

The dining room was crowded. Feeling a battery of eyes upon her, Andrea was grateful when Stuart took her hand in his, not realising what a handsome pair they made. It was fine for him to tell her not to feel shy, she thought, but somehow sharing breakfast with him seemed much more intimate than having dinner with him.

Afterwards they walked from the hotel to a nearby sports store where Stuart knew they could rent skates. The air was crisp and clear with a touch of frost and it felt good to be alive. Stuart had been right, she mused; she had allowed her accident to poison her whole outlook on life and she had been living in a kind of dreadful vacuum for far too long. Yet as the salesman lifted the gleaming white boots from the box, she could not control the tremor in her fingers as she removed her shoes. Stuart loosened the laces and knelt before her, easing her slender foot into the white leather, his eyes steady on her face in an unspoken message of reassurance. She stood up, gingerly putting her weight on her foot. 'That feels fine,' she said, a double message in the simple words.

Stuart paid for the skates and they walked back to the hotel to get the car. The school was on the outskirts of Calgary, its cluster of red brick buildings surrounded by lawns from which most of the snow had melted. Bare-limbed trees lined the driveway.

Stuart parked the car, got out, and walked round to her side to open the door. Her lips felt dry. She licked them, knowing suddenly that she was nervous of meeting his children for the first time. What if they didn't like her? As though he had read her thoughts, Stuart said, 'Don't worry, they'll like you.'

The headmaster met them at the door.

'Good morning, Mr Trent. Heather and Bruce are anxious to see you.' With polite curiosity he eyed Stuart's companion.

'Good morning, Mr Sheldon. I'd like you to meet a friend of mine, Miss Andrea MacKinlay. Andrea, this is Tom Sheldon.'

'How do you do, Miss MacKinlay. Please follow me, the children are in the lounge.'

Andrea hesitated in the doorway, not wanting to intrude on Stuart's reunion with his children. She had no difficulty recognising them, for they were the children of the photograph, though older now, and dressed in neat school uniforms with their hair tidily combed. They had been sitting primly on the sofa, but as they saw their father, they could not restrain themselves any longer and ran to meet him. He stooped, gathering one in each arm. The three black heads so close together tugged at Andrea's heartstrings, while an unbidden lump came to her throat. Stuart was laughing as he tried to sort out the flood of incomprehensible chatter that poured forth from the two excited children. Heather had both arms about his neck in a stranglehold, her clear treble piping, 'We've missed you, Daddy.' Bruce, as befitted a boy, stood sturdily at his father's side, but his small fingers were clutching the heavy wool sweater, as though he were afraid his father would disappear. 'Are we going skating?' he asked.

'Of course we are!' Stuart replied. 'And I've brought a friend to go with us.' He got to his feet, the two children still holding tightly to him. 'Come here, Andrea.' She walked slowly across the room, her only thought how absurdly like their father the children were, miniature replicas of his dark good looks.

'This is Andrea MacKinlay, children. Andrea, meet Heather and Bruce.'

The two little faces smiled at her. 'You're pretty,' said Heather admiringly.

'Do you know how to skate?' demanded Bruce with his father's masculine forthrightness.

'Well, thank you, Heather, I think you're pretty too. And yes, Bruce, I do know how to skate,' she replied softly as her eyes met Stuart's in a look of perfect understanding.

'That's my girl!' he murmured.

Even so, when Stuart pushed open the door of the rink, Andrea's new-found confidence quailed. The air was cold. Music was playing and from the ice came the shrieks of excited children, although most of the tiered seats were empty. Sight, smell, and sound . . . all combined to carry her back into the past. She closed her eyes, wondering if she was going to be able to go through with this after all.

'This is the hardest part, Andrea,' said Stuart's deep voice in her ear. 'Keep your chin up. Let's get the children's skates on first.'

Glad of the diversion, Andrea did as she was told, and watched smilingly as the children staggered on to the ice. Almost before she knew it Stuart had laced up her own skates. She waited for him, feeling the dampness on the palms of her hands. He intertwined her ice-cold fingers with his and led her down the wooden steps and out on the ice. She staggered as a small body cannoned into her, and Heather grabbed her other hand.

'Come on, Daddy,' the little girl shrieked, 'Let's all go around together!'

Stuart reached out for his son. In a somewhat erratic fashion the four of them skated around the rink, Andrea so busy trying to keep Heather upright that she had no time to feel nervous. For half an hour she and Stuart played with the children before he said, 'Andrea and I are going to skate for a while now—don't break your necks, you two.'

Their arms about each other, they circled the rink, weaving in and out of the other skaters with increasing sureness. He looked down at her. 'Having fun?' he asked.

With complete truth she was able to answer in the affirmative. Suddenly his supporting arm was gone, as he said, 'It looks as though Bruce needs a hand. I'll be back in a minute.'

She faltered momentarily as his broad back moved away from her. But then the rhythm of the music and the discipline of her long years of training reasserted themselves and once again her blades bit firmly into the ice. In a trance of rediscovered delight she forgot her surroundings and the other skaters; she became one with the music and with herself. Almost without realising it, she repeated many of the movements of her old programme, gliding, leaping, and spinning with increasing confidence. It was a physical shock when the music stopped and reality returned. Embarrassed, she heard a ripple of applause from the assembled children and parents. Wanting only to be anonymous, she skated quickly over to Stuart, Heather and Bruce.

'Wow! You're a great skater!' the little boy exclaimed.

'Will you teach me how to do some of those things?' Heather asked, her blue eyes big with wonder.

'That was beautiful, Andrea,' Stuart said quietly. 'How do you feel?'

She tipped back her head and laughed, a cascade of pure joy. 'Oh, Stuart,' she cried, 'that was marvellous! You have no idea how good it felt.' Abruptly she sobered, and added with desperate sincerity, 'I can never thank you enough.'

'I'm hungry, Daddy,' Bruce interrupted. 'Can we eat now?'

'You're always hungry, chum,' Stuart laughed, his hand

affectionately ruffling his son's black hair. 'But I guess that's a good idea. How about you, Andrea?'

'To tell the truth, I'm ravenous,' she chuckled.

'That settles it. Let's go.'

Several hours later they began their journey back to the ranch. Before they had left the city limits, both children had fallen into an exhausted slumber in the back seat. Andrea leaned back and tucked the car rug around their legs.

'They're worn out,' she whispered to her companion.

'It was a good day, wasn't it?' he smiled.

And so it had been. At lunch time the children had consumed unbelievably vast quantities of hamburgers, french fries and ice cream, which had not prevented them from munching on popcorn during a theatre matinee! Andrea could remember the feeling of being a part of a close-knit family that had developed during the course of the afternoon; she was sure that other people had believed them to be husband and wife, parents of Heather and Bruce; and a part of her was beginning to wish it was so.

They had all dressed for dinner at the hotel, and it had given Andrea intense pleasure to brush Heather's glossy curls and to help her button her long dress. She herself had worn the dinner dress again, but with what different feelings from the night before! She had been proud of the children's behaviour and delighted by how easily they had accepted her.

'A penny for them,' Stuart said.

'I was just thinking what a good day it's been,' she said. 'A good day from beginning to end,' she added, knowing he would understand that she was thanking him again for the support he had given her that morning.

He reached out an arm and pulled her closer to him. 'Tired?' he asked.

'Mmmm,' she murmured, letting her head rest against his shoulder.

'Your hair smells nice,' he whispered. 'I was proud of you this morning. You've laid a ghost to rest, haven't you?'

She nodded, knowing that she had. An unbidden thought

flashed across her mind: if only she could banish the ghost of his dead wife as easily. Then her eyes closed, her lashes thick against her pale skin, and she drifted off to sleep.

She did not awaken until she felt the car turn off the main highway and on to the dirt road leading to his house. 'Are we home already?' she enquired sleepily.

'Nearly there.'

As she slept, one hand had fallen across his thigh. Glad that the darkness could hide the sudden warmth that rose to her face, she twisted away from him to look at the children in the back seat. 'They're still sleeping.'

The headlights of the car pierced the blackness in front of them, picking out the outlines of trees and shrubs along the road. The sky was a velvet black, spangled with distant stars—return to silence and the peace of open space.

'Cities are exciting, but somehow this is more real,' she said.

'Most young women don't feel that way,' he said, with a violence out of all proportion to her simple statement. 'But I couldn't agree with you more.'

'Well, I guess I'm not like most young women, then,' she said defensively.

'I'm beginning to think you're not.'

Not sure of the cause or the motive behind the conversation, she was saved from the necessity of a reply when the car drew up in front of the house. Even as deserted and dark as it was, she felt as though she had come home.

'Wait a second until I unlock the door and turn on a few lights, and then I'll carry the children in,' said Stuart. He returned in a few minutes and gathered his daughter into his arms, Andrea trailing up the stairs behind him. Heather's bedroom was as pretty as any little girl could want, with its frilly net curtains and flowered carpet. As Stuart put the child down on the bed, Andrea suggested, 'I'll undress her and get her into bed, so you can go and get Bruce.'

In short order they had both children tucked in bed. 'I'll start the fire and put the kettle on, if you want to change into something warmer,' he offered.

She got a sweater from her drawer, for the house had struck chilly. To her surprise the living room was deserted and in darkness, but from the study came the crackle of a friendly fire. Andrea entered the study, which had always been her favourite room in the house, and gracefully sank down on the sheepskin rug in front of the hearth, pulling two of the brightly coloured cushions to support her back. She gazed into the flames, hypnotised by their orange brilliance, not realising that Stuart was standing by the door watching her. The firelight flickered and danced, its glow reflecting on her creamy skin, her eyes mysterious pools of darkness. As relaxed and sensuous as a cat, she leaned her head back on the pillows, exposing the slender length of her throat, the soft swell of her breasts outlined against the flames.

Her first inkling that he had joined her was the chink of glass against the hearth. Startled, her eyelashes flew upwards.

'Don't move,' he said, and lowered his lean body to sit beside her. 'I hope you like Irish coffee.'

'I've never had it before.'

He touched his glass to hers and they drank. The coffee was piping hot and laced with whiskey; with the tip of her tongue Andrea licked the cream from her top lip. 'It's delicious,' she said, very much aware of his grey eyes intent upon her face and of the flames leaping in their depths. He took the glass from her unresisting hand and placed it carefully on the hearth. Her breath caught in her throat as he pulled her body to his, lowering them both gently to the floor, her hair spread in a silken tangle on the cushion. He pressed his mouth to hers in a kiss of deep hunger and restrained passion.

Her body melted into his with an answering hunger she had never felt before. Her lips parted under the force of his kiss, as with every fibre of her being she felt the weight of his thighs against hers. The hardness of his chest pushed her against the pillow, as he buried his face in her neck, inhaling the scented sweetness of her skin. Her back arched and her arms encircled his body, her fingers digging into the muscled smoothness of his back. Swept by a torrent of desire, she murmured his name against his throat, 'Oh, Stuart . . .'

'Andrea, my beautiful Andrea,' he groaned. His hand was beneath her blouse, caressing the warm skin of her back.

With a suddenness that made her cry out, he pulled away so that she fell back against the cushion. Her eyes, huge with questioning, searched his tortured face. 'What's wrong?' she faltered.

'Nothing and everything,' he muttered.

'Did I do something wrong?' she repeated, tears stinging at her eyelids.

'Oh God, no, Andrea!' he exclaimed. 'It was I who nearly did something wrong. I would never have forgiven myself if I had . . . you're so young and innocent, and far too desirable for my peace of mind.'

He stood and turned his back to her. 'I think you'd better go to bed now,' he said huskily.

She reached out a hand to him in supplication, but dropped it to her side. In futility, feeling like a naughty child who had been dismissed from his presence, she walked from the study.

Alone in her room she undressed slowly, while questions whirled in her head. Would she ever understand Stuart Trent? He had said that she was beautiful and desirable, and that he wanted her—but he had not said that he loved her. 'Love' . . . a simple one-syllable word with so many implications.

She stood still, staring at her pale reflection in the mirror. The word 'love' had struck her like a blow. Out of the confusion that claimed her mind came the sure realisation that she loved Stuart, loved him with all the strength and tenderness of which she was capable.

It was a realisation of mingled happiness and despair, for Stuart was a man haunted by his past and she, Andrea, could not fight a ghost. His dead wife had so strong a hold on him that he was not free to love again, and perhaps never would be.

Andrea gave a sharp sigh. So this was love, this pain that gripped her heart, this longing that cut her like a knife. She had in the past imagined herself falling in love, and had painted a rosy picture of joy and laughter and sharing. The reality was far removed from her fantasy. But it was a reality, she knew; she loved Stuart whatever happened, loved him irrevocably.

CHAPTER FOUR

ANDREA was awakened the next morning by the happy sounds of childish laughter and by springing vibrations on her bed. Her sleep had not been a restful one and as soon as she woke, she painfully recalled the events of the previous evening. She shifted her body slightly and slowly opened her eyes, to see Heather with laughter lighting her small face, a face that in an instant achingly reminded Andrea of Stuart's. Heather leapt with joyful abandon at the end of Andrea's bed.

'Come on, Andrea, you jump too!' she pleaded, excitement lilting in her voice.

Andrea propped her arms behind her head and gazed at the little girl, then said in serious tones, 'Oh, no, Heather, not me. I would probably break the bed. Or else I might hit my head on the ceiling, bounce right out through my window, and end up on the lawn.'

'You're teasing, I know you really wouldn't do that,' Heather giggled as she continued her brief journeys into the space immediately above Andrea's bed. Her silky black curls flung themselves outward from her face with each leap. 'Anyway,' she continued, 'we're hungry, Bruce and me, and Daddy's still in bed. He never sleeps this late. Can't we have breakfast now? I'm starved and Bruce is frumished, I know he is . . . he always is . . . and sometimes I get frumished too. You come and get us breakfast, Andrea.' All this as she continued a steady rhythm of leaping on Andrea's bed. Finally she stopped, out of breath, but only for the moment.

'So you're hungry and on your way to being "frumished" are you, darling? I think I have a touch of being "frumished" too,' said Andrea teasingly. 'Get Bruce and we'll see what we can put together in the kitchen.'

Andrea gathered her warm robe around her and put on

her slippers, then left her room and walked quietly down the stairs. The house was silent. She paused for a moment at the door of the study, letting her gaze rest on the cushions still lying on the floor and on the now dead and charred embers in the fireplace. A wave of despair washed over her. What was she going to do? How could she continue to work in this house, so near to him and yet so utterly divided from him? He must not know how she felt; he must never guess the truth. That would truly be more than she could bear. With firm resolution she forced herself to walk on to the kitchen.

Heather and Bruce came running in behind her, pushing past her, each in a rush to be the first one at the table.

'Hold on you two, I know you're both "frumished" as you put it, but that's no way to act. There's room for both of you at this table and then some, so slow down a bit.'

'What's for breakfast, Andrea?' asked Heather.

'Is it ready yet?' questioned Bruce eagerly.

'I got here *after* you both, if you care to recall,' grinned Andrea, 'so obviously it isn't ready yet. Now what would you like?'

'Hot dogs and french fries,' Bruce interjected seriously.

'Yes, that's a really good idea, that's what we want ... hot dogs and french fries ... we never have them for breakfast at school,' Heather added with equal sobriety.

'Well, you're not going to have them here either, my young miss and master—yuk, what a terrible thought!' Andrea grimaced. 'How about griddle cakes?'

'Oh yes, we like them. Make lots and lots. Daddy likes them too, so make extra lots and lots and then we can give Daddy his breakfast in bed,' Heather pleaded.

Andrea prepared their breakfast. Piping hot griddle cakes, with whipped butter melting succulently on the top, and maple syrup glistening in brown pools. The children ate quickly, asking for second helpings as Andrea had guessed they would.

'Slow down, you'll get the hiccups,' warned Andrea, who had finished hers and was lazily sipping a cup of hot coffee.

'We'll take Daddy's up to him now. Let's go, Bruce,' said

Heather, getting quickly down from her chair.

'Hold it. Drink your milk and don't gulp it and I'll fix the tray.'

It was obvious to Andrea that the two children couldn't carry the tray alone, for as Heather picked it up, the coffee mug was sliding around dangerously, threatening to totter over the side. So Andrea took the tray and followed the children upstairs. They opened the door to their father's room. Andrea's heart beat wildly at the sight of him, this man who had become so dear to her in such a short time. She could feel warmth creep into her face. How vulnerable he seemed lying there in the midst of the disarray of crumpled sheets and blankets. Her eyes lingered on the dark head, tousled curls framing his tanned face that now showed none of the tortured lines of last night. One arm lay lightly across his chest, his other arm was outstretched across the bed. The lean muscular figure stirred slightly. He opened his eyes and slowly turned to the three figures filling the doorframe. In an instant the children burst noisily into the room, running and climbing on to the bed. They descended upon him, rolling over his body with all the fervour and abandon of two puppies at play.

He held them away from him for a moment, the strength in his arms obvious, and his eyes met Andrea's in a searching glance. She saw on his face a look that she could not understand . . . a slight narrowing of the eyes . . . an almost imperceptible darkening. He was obviously thinking that she had no right to be here in the intimacy of his bedroom, that she was an unwelcome intruder. The warmth glowed on her cheeks once again and she thought desperately, he must not learn how I feel; he must never guess the truth.

In order to prevent any hint of her true feelings escaping, she spoke to him in a biting tone, precision sharpening the cut of every word. 'The children wanted to bring you your breakfast in bed. They couldn't manage the tray by themselves, so I carried it up for them. Where would you like it, Mr Trent?'

She saw that her words had the effect she desired. His face darkened and he said coolly, 'Over on the desk for now, please ... Andrea.' For some unknown reason he had refused to follow her example in the use of her name.

She placed the tray on the desk as he had directed and walked stiffly from the room, saying only as she closed the door, 'I'll leave you alone with your children.'

She left him no time for a response of any nature, afraid to learn what it might be. This was going to be so much more difficult than she had supposed, but she knew she dared not falter: he must not learn her secret.

Standing outside his room she heard the shrill giggling of the children and the deep laughter of their father, who so obviously loved them. But if he loved them so much, as he seemed to, why then did he choose to have them with him for only short periods of the year? There were so many things that she could not comprehend about this man Stuart Trent, she thought with exasperation.

Andrea went to her room, tidied it, and made the bed. After she had showered and put on her grey slacks and a crisp tailored white blouse, she went to the children's rooms and made their beds, thinking to herself that Heather and Bruce were old enough to care for their own rooms, and to be helping around the house, by doing the dishes, for example. Learning about the care of their own home would be good for them, would teach them responsibility and would also help them to develop a sense of pride in what was theirs. She should, she supposed, speak to Stuart about it.

As she passed Stuart's room the children scampered past her and down the stairs. She heard Stuart's strong voice call to her, 'Andrea, come here, please.' It was not a request, it was a command. Although her first impulse was to walk past, ignoring it, she knew that this was impossible. After all, she was in his employ. She returned to the entrance of his room and waited without comment for whatever he further wished to say.

He stood there, naked to the waist, tight-fitting brown cord trousers revealing the muscular strength and power of his thighs and legs.

'You didn't sleep well last night?' he queried, carefully scrutinising her face.

'I slept very well, Mr Trent, thank you,' she lied in a crisp tone.

He turned sharply, the steel glint in his dark eyes threatening to cut through her assumed composure. He threw the shirt he was holding on the bed. 'What in the hell is this "Mr Trent" business? You act as if . . .' He did not finish, for Andrea interrupted him abruptly.

'We need to get a few things straight, or to keep a few things straight perhaps.' Her throat tightened and for a moment she felt that she could not continue, but she pushed on. 'I let myself forget that you are my employer, and I am your employee. That's all—nothing more.'

He had been standing by the window listening intently to her words. Seeing that she had finished, he came towards her, his hand reaching out for her, but she backed away from him. 'Don't come near me!' She paused. 'Don't touch me.' Choosing her words with some difficulty, she continued sharply, 'I'll keep your house in order, cooking and cleaning for you until Maggie returns. Then I shall do your typing as we previously arranged . . . unless you have no further need of me in that capacity.'

He stood still, his face hard as if carved from stone, his eyes dark with anger. 'Thank you . . . Miss MacKinlay,' he muttered with more than a slight hint of sarcasm. 'I appreciate and accept your offer to act in the capacity of housekeeper until Maggie comes back. Of course, I shall expect you to spend some time entertaining the children as well. Afterwards, you need only to fulfil the functions of a typist—I shall expect nothing more from you . . . nothing.' He uttered this last word with a grating harshness that tore at the thin armour she had constructed.

He did not wait for a response from her, but ended their exchange by saying in a low voice, 'You may go now . . . and tend to your duties.' He turned from her, reaching for the shirt he had flung across the bed and putting it on.

Once more she had been dismissed by him. Anger rose

visibly in her face, but she stopped herself from verbalising it, instead marching efficiently from the room. After all, she told herself, this was what she had wanted, what she had demanded ... to be his employee, nothing more. She felt scant comfort in the fact that he had so swiftly, and with so obvious little caring, granted her wish.

Andrea had just finished cleaning Stuart's study when the phone rang. Startled for a moment by its sharp demanding tone, she hesitated to answer. Realising that she should perhaps count that as one of her tasks as housekeeper, she moved to pick up the receiver, just as Stuart strode into the room and answered it himself. Whatever the content of the conversation, the fact that it was a source of frustration was made plain by the scowl on his face. She was about to excuse herself when Stuart placed his hand over the receiver and stated tersely, 'Perhaps you would spend some time with the children now, Miss Mac-Kinlay. And close the door on your way out, please, I don't want to be disturbed.' Andrea, struggling to conceal her unhappiness, nodded and left.

She and the twins dressed warmly and went out for a ramble around the main house. It was a bitterly cold day, not at all what Andrea expected from the month of April; the wind was cutting and she wished she had worn mittens. Within her she did not feel the promise of spring was going to be kept.

But being with the children and watching their childish pleasure in the things around them was good, and she soon became absorbed in their activities. She enjoyed the undisguised delight on Heather's face at the sight of the new kittens in the barn, and marvelled at Bruce's total lack of timidity with the huge stallion. He seemed to have a good deal of Stuart's quiet strength even in these early years.

Heather was playing with the kittens and Bruce was murmuring affectionately to the horses when Stuart entered the barn. Andrea did not see him at first, and she jumped at the touch of his hand on her shoulder. He quickly withdrew his hand, and not looking at her moved over to Heather. 'I just came to see how you three were getting on,' he said.

'Oh, Daddy, come and see the kittens, they're so soft and cuddly!'

Stuart knelt down beside her, his long fingers stroking the tiny head of one of the kittens. Andrea watched him, seeing the gentleness of his touch, amazed that so large a man should possess it to such a degree.

'I'm glad you like them, sweetheart; they are lovely, aren't they?' he said quietly. 'Look at this one—it's striped like a little tiger.' Then he got up and walked over to Bruce. 'Want to go for a ride with me, son?' he asked.

Bruce looked disbelievingly at his father. 'Really, Dad? You mean right now?'

Stuart nodded.

'Oh yes! I want to, for sure.'

With long firm strokes Stuart groomed the stallion until the chestnut coat shone. Then he saddled and bridled the horse, explaining to Bruce how the bit worked and how to tighten the girth. Afterwards, he lifted Bruce easily into the saddle, lithely swinging himself up behind the boy. His arms encircled his son, as his body shielded him protectively. The stallion, guided expertly out of the barn, broke into an easy lope, heading down the road to the ranch buildings.

Heather watched, saying excitedly, 'Daddy promised to get us ponies this summer, Andrea—won't that be fun? Then we can all go together. Why don't you take me on Star now? We could catch up to Bruce and Daddy and surprise them.'

'I'm sorry, honey, but I can't ride that well. To be honest, I just can't ride at all,' admitted Andrea.

'Well, Daddy'll fix that, he'll teach you. He's a great rider,' said his daughter confidently.

Andrea could see that Stuart was indeed an expert horseman, as at home on a horse as she had been on skates. She and Heather walked slowly along the road, the bitter wind lashing their faces, so that their eyes watered from the sting.

'Don't you think we should head back to the house now, Heather?' Andrea suggested. 'It's getting colder by the minute. I think we need a hot lunch to thaw us out.'

Heather nodded in agreement, slipping her small hand into Andrea's. 'Yes—let's run!' she exclaimed, tugging Andrea along with her.

Back in the warmth of the house, Andrea heated some of the home-made soup that Maggie had left for them. She mixed a pan of tea biscuits, put them in the oven, and set the table for four, listening to Heather's voice chatter on with a vivacity that seemed to be a natural state for the little girl. 'Daddy's going to take us up on the chair-lift this afternoon, Andrea, he promised this morning. It's going to be such a good vacation, and soon we'll be home for the *whole* summer!'

Andrea turned and looked at the little girl. 'You really miss your father when you're away at school, don't you, Heather?'

'Oh yes. I wish we could stay with him here all the time ... for ever and ever,' Heather replied wistfully, stretching out her arms to show Andrea just how long 'for ever and ever' looked. 'Ever since Barbara left, we've lived at the school, except for vacations. Daddy says it's better for us there.'

'You must miss your mother very much too, darling,' Andrea said, looking tenderly down at the small innocent face.

But Heather had no chance to reply. Their conversation ended there, for Bruce burst into the room. 'Daddy's coming in a minute, he's putting Shah back in the barn.' His face was red from the wind and from the excitement of the ride with his father. 'Mr Roberts came back with us. I think he's gonna stay for lunch too.'

Lunch proved to be a relaxing time for Andrea and the children, who took no pains to hide their admiration of Clayton Roberts. The ranch hand was easily six feet tall, with broad and muscled shoulders—a big man, nearly as tall as Stuart. However, in contrast to Stuart's curly black hair, Clayton's was a startling pure white. His face was tanned and leathery, a result of long exposure to the sun and the wind and the rain; he looked to be in his early fifties. In effect, as Andrea later found out to her amazement, he was sixty. He had deep blue eyes, the colour of sky in winter, which were gently touched at the edges by wrinkles that revealed a deep appreciation of laughter. He was a tough and capable man, that was obvious, and yet there was something calm and peaceful about him too, as if here was a man who had come to know himself fully—who knew what it was he wanted from life ... had found it ... and had kept it.

'You're a real cowboy, aren't you, Mr Roberts?' Bruce said. 'You've got a gun, haven't you?' On and on the questions came, questions that left no time for answers. Answers were not necessary to Bruce, for the boy had, in his own young mind, a firmly established image of Clayton Roberts.

Stuart was withdrawn and quiet during lunch, letting the children dominate the conversation. When he finished eating he got up from the table, excused himself and spoke briefly to Clayton, 'I'll meet with you in the study when you're ready, Clayton.' He turned to Heather and Bruce and added, 'I'm sorry, kids, but the chair-lift is out for this afternoon. I'm expecting an important call from New York that I've got to be here for. It's really too cold to go anyway.' He said nothing to Andrea and he did not look at her as he left the kitchen.

Andrea shared the children's disappointment. In addition, she was angry with Stuart for his summary dismissal of their plans; Heather and Bruce had such a short period at home, that the least he could do was spend as much time as possible with them. But no, it was first things first with him, and the play clearly superseded the children's needs—she, Andrea, could not agree with his priorities.

The rest of the week passed quite swiftly, although neither Andrea nor the children saw much of Stuart. He was apparently rewriting a scene of the play, as a result of a number of phone calls he had received from New York. At the end of the week he asked Andrea to type the work he had rewritten.

'I'm sorry, Miss MacKinlay, I realise this is asking for more than we agreed, but I'll pay you for the extra work,' he said formally. 'Do you think you can complete this tonight?'

She nodded, accepting the papers with a terse, 'I'll do my best.'

'I'll see that you're not disturbed. I can put the children to bed,' he added brusquely.

When she had completed the manuscript, Andrea took it to Stuart's study. His desk was scattered with papers; he was seated in the deep leather chair behind it, turned at an angle away from the desk, staring through the window into the blackness beyond, his long body motionless. To the watching girl he looked isolated and lonely; she longed to reach out and touch him and to feel his touch. Steeling herself against such treacherous desires, she moved towards him, the sound of her approach finally penetrating his abstraction. He turned to look at her, his face not revealing any of his thoughts or feelings. He stood up to accept the papers she held out to him, his hand brushing against hers for one electrifying second. She quickly withdrew her fingers, as if she had been stung. He must have seen this reaction, but made no comment other than a businesslike, 'Thank you, you've been very prompt.'

'Are Heather and Bruce settled?' Andrea questioned.

'Yes, they were quite tired, they've been asleep for an hour or so now,' he responded dully.

Andrea said nothing more, wanting only to escape to the silent refuge of her own room. Turning to leave, however, she was stopped by his voice continuing in the same lifeless tone. 'The children tell me that you're taking them shopping and to the library in Valleyfield tomorrow afternoon. Would you mind mailing the revised manuscript for me while you're there?'

She turned on him suddenly and angrily retorted, 'They're your children, Stuart Trent, why don't you take them to town yourself, and mail that precious manuscript yourself!' Now that she had started, all the resentment that had been building up over the past few days exploded to the surface. 'For heaven's sake, spend a little more time with them! They love you so much—more than you deserve—and they need you. They certainly need more of your company than you've seen fit to share with them this week. Which is more important to you—your play or your children?'

She stopped. She had gone too far, the words spilling out without censor, her body shaking with emotion. She nearly began to apologise and say she had spoken out of turn, but the undisguised anger in his face and voice cut through her and silenced any words she had been about to utter.

'What do you expect from me?' he demanded, his breathing tight and controlled. He came around the end of the desk, his huge frame towering over her. 'I do as much as I can for them. I give them as much time as I can spare. I can't do any more than that, can I?'

'As much time as you can spare is about right,' she retorted. 'And precious little it is. I can see your priorities very plainly . . . and so can your son and daughter.'

'What the hell do you mean by that?'

'Just because they're only eight years old, it doesn't mean they don't realise what's going on.'

'They're well cared for. They're loved, and they know it.'

'Then why don't they live with you .. always ... not just for a few weeks of the year? But of course I can answer that question, can't I? That's all the time you can spare them. Forgive me if I don't applaud your generosity.'

He came towards her, his face pale, his hands clenched into white-knuckled fists. For a moment she thought he was going to strike her, but as if tottering on the edge of a precipice, he drew back, releasing a long harsh breath.

'What's the use of trying to explain to you anyway, Andrea? You aren't listening! You choose not to listen, not to try and understand my side of it, no matter what I have to say.' Of what his voice had verbally accused her, so had

his eyes at this point. Nevertheless, for one swift moment
Andrea thought that she saw in their dark depths an
almost tortured plea. But that was foolish, and she dismissed her misinterpretation as quickly as it had arisen,
giving him only a careless shrug. He said no more to her
but turned abruptly and walked from the room, slamming
the door forcibly behind him.

Stuart did not eat with them at breakfast the next
morning, for he had risen early, saddled the stallion, and
had gone with Clayton to check on some range cattle. This
Andrea learned from the children. Later in the morning,
taking the sealed and stamped manuscript with her, she
drove Heather and Bruce into Valleyfield. Despite a restless
night that resulted in little sleep, and the cold cloudy
weather, she enjoyed being with the children. She admitted
to herself that she had grown more than fond of these two
innocent and loveable creatures, so like and yet so unlike
their father. Her strained relationship with Stuart was
torturing her; things had worsened with last night's argument.

Perhaps when the children returned to school in Calgary, it would be time for her to leave too. It was obvious
Stuart did not need her, since Maggie would be coming
back next week, and he could surely find another typist.
Yet how could she leave him? She needed to be near him,
she loved him so desperately. Yes, it was a desperate love,
shadowed as it was by a dead wife he could not forget, who
would not allow him to love another woman. Although
Andrea knew he found her attractive and desirable, he had
never said, even in their closest moments, that he loved
her.

She sighed. No matter how he treated her, no matter
how badly it hurt, she had to stay. She was honest enough
to admit to herself that she lacked the courage to leave
him. The mere thought of never seeing him again opened
before her a black void, a vision of a life of meaningless
and futile hours. She was trapped, trapped by her own
ungovernable emotions, in a situation which could yield her
nothing but further pain.

Andrea pushed thoughts of Stuart from her mind and turned her full attention to Heather and Bruce. They ate a cheerful lunch at the hotel, did a little shopping, and spent some time at the library, both the children choosing books to take home with them.

Only one thing happened to mar the enjoyment of the afternoon. They had been walking along the sidewalk towards the spot where Andrea had parked the Mercedes when Bruce uttered a cry of pleasure. Parked at the curb in front of the drug store was a bright yellow Jaguar. Bruce ran over to the car, gingerly running his small hands along its sleek side.

'Wow, Andrea! Just look at this! Isn't it something! Some day I'm gonna have one just like this. I'll bet it can go a hundred and fifty, I'll bet it can really go!'

Bending down to look at it, watching the boy's bubbling excitement, her eyes fell on two figures standing in front of the store directly across the street. Her heart skipped a beat. She straightened quickly and called sharply to the children to hurry along, herding them towards the Mercedes. The two people were Ronald Martin and his mother; the last people she wanted to see. Once in the car she breathed a sigh of relief, thankful that they hadn't seen her. She would have been surprised to know that Ronald had in fact seen her, and had watched her carefully through narrowed and interested eyes. He had also recognised the twins as Stuart's children, for at one time, granted for only a short time, he had known Barbara Trent ... very well.

That evening Andrea retired early, choosing the privacy of her own room rather than another stress-filled evening of strained conversation with Stuart. She read to the children, tucked them in bed, and walked quietly along the thickly carpeted hallway to her bedroom, which now seemed so peaceful and protected a haven. Outside the wind had increased in fury and a few snowflakes were falling; Stuart had said at supper that a storm warning had been issued. Andrea could not believe that April would be the month to harbour such an occurrence, but as she gazed from her window down towards the flickering lights of the bunkhouse about a mile away, she sensed an unleashing of nature's powers, a gathering of forces beyond human control.

Feeling tired and heavy-eyed, she read for only a few minutes before falling into a deep sleep, an escape from the tensions of the past few days.

She was dreaming ... it was scarcely daylight and she was being shaken, a hand rough and warm on her bare shoulder. She tried to push it away, murmuring, 'Go away, it's not morning yet.' But a hand fell on her other shoulder and she was being pulled to an upright position.

She blinked her eyes, pushing her silky hair off her face with her fingers, and confusedly focusing on Stuart's face, barely a foot from hers. It was his hands that were gripping her naked flesh, and his voice that she now realised was repeating something for the third time. 'Where are the children?' he demanded.

'What do you mean?' she asked drowsily, trying to adjust her eyes to the light. 'Where are the children? In their beds, of course, where else would they be at this hour?'

'Well, they're not in their beds,' he said roughly, 'and they're nowhere else in the house, because I've looked. I thought that maybe they might have been afraid of the storm and come into bed with you ...' his voice trailed off into private thoughts. 'God help them if they've gone out in this.'

Fully awake, she stared at him, horror-stricken. 'Gone out? Oh, Stuart, they couldn't have!' For now she could hear the angry shriek of the wind, the lash of ice pellets against the window.

'They're nowhere in the house, Andrea.'

'Did you check the back porch to see if their snowsuits are hanging up there?'

'Hell, no. I'm not thinking straight. I'll go and look right now.'

She pushed aside the blankets and swung her legs out of bed, not even thinking of the scantiness of her thin nylon nightdress. 'I'll get dressed and come and help you look.'

For one split second his glance raked her from head to toe. The animosity between them had vanished, banished by the threat of the missing children. He gave her a quick hug, crushing her against his lean length, and she felt his lips fall on her hair. 'Good girl. I'll meet you downstairs. Dress warmly.'

She pulled on jeans and a heavy sweater, then raced down the stairs, praying that the two green snowsuits would be in their usual place. But in the front porch she found Stuart staring numbly at two empty hooks. 'They're gone,' he said blankly.

'Maybe the children were worried about the kittens in the storm,' she suggested helplessly.

'I'll go and check.'

'I'm coming with you,' she said in a tone that allowed no argument.

He gave her none, instead throwing his sheepskin jacket at her. 'Put that on, I'll wear my parka. Come on, hurry!'

As he opened the door, an icy blast of blowing snow tore through her sweater to her skin. She had to lean her body into the blinding white sheet to even remain standing. Unsure if she could last for long in this unbelievable chaos of wind and snow, she pushed herself forward, straining every muscle and fibre of mind and body to keep up with Stuart.

They made it to the stables, the wind slamming the door shut behind them. But the children were not to be found in the sweet-smelling gloom. Stuart shook his head helplessly. 'Andrea, where could they have gone? How can we find them in this? We can't even see a foot in front of us. And if we don't find them soon . . .' He was shouting over the screaming of the wind, but he did not finish the last sentence.

Even in her anxiety she found time to be pleased by his use of the pronoun 'we'. Clutching his arm, and remembering the time he had found her in just such another storm, she shouted, 'The jeep! Why don't we take the jeep?'

'It's worth a try . . . it's something. I'll go back to the

house, call Clayton, and tell him to get the men out to help search. Wait here, I'll be right back.' He opened the door of the barn and pushed himself out into the storm, the gale howling with a murderous violence she had not believed possible.

He returned shortly with the jeep, the hood and sides of the windshield already piled high with snow. She ploughed through the drifts towards him, hearing him yell out to her, 'The phone's out! I couldn't get through to Clayton. We'll have to drive down. Get in!'

It was difficult driving. Andrea strained to see the edge of the road, to discover some indication that they were at least heading in the right direction. But she could not distinguish anything outside the jeep. She felt as though she were being swallowed alive by a voracious white monster, a monster that had already stolen her vision, replacing it by a blank whirl of whiteness. A searing fear suffocated her, closing her throat and almost preventing her from breathing. She and Stuart were lost in a world of unknown but deadly menace. And somewhere in this same world were lost the children they both loved. Heather and Bruce ... she prayed that they had not been destroyed by an uncaring act of nature, a freak storm. Her mind reacted to the thought in raging denial. They would find the children—they must find them!

She turned to look at Stuart. His eyes, unblinking, stared out ... at ... at what? At the white, because that was all there was. How could he know he was heading in the right direction? His mouth was tight, his jaw rigid. His hands grasped the wheel with the same white-knuckled pressure she had seen when he had been so angry with her. But now, he was not angry, he was desperately worried and tense, only too aware that in this country, in this weather, time was the essence. If Heather and Bruce were to be saved, they would have to find them soon ... if it was not already too late.

She was wondering again at his seemingly uncanny sense of direction, wondering if in fact he too might not feel lost, when the grey outline of the bunkhouse filtered into view, faded white as if it were photographed through a piece of gauze or cheesecloth.

A deep relief suffused her. At least now they would have the help of Clayton and the ranch hands. She felt a surge of admiration for Stuart's ability to keep the jeep on a road she could not even see.

But as this thought brushed her mind, the jeep slid sideways. Stuart swung the wheel with the skid, but the vehicle didn't respond. With grim-jawed concentration he accelerated in an attempt to drive out of it. Neither action worked. The jeep careened into an unseen ditch, Andrea being thrown forward, striking her forehead on the dash with painful force. Fighting to catch her breath and stop the darkness that was closing in on her, she heard Stuart speak. He seemed to be so far away, his voice such a long distance from her, that she had to strain to hear his faint words.

'Andrea? Are you all right? Are you hurt?'

'No. I'm fine,' she reassured him, momentarily winning the battle for consciousness and not wanting to delay him further. 'What do we do now?'

'We get out and walk. The bunkhouse is just ahead,' he directed. Because the jeep was on its side in the ditch, she had to clamber over Stuart's side to get out. He half lifted and half pulled her out into the storm. She closed her eyes to avoid the stinging onrush of driven snow. Stuart took her hand, partly guiding and partially dragging her along with him. Just when she felt that she could not continue, not even if her life depended on it, they reached the safety and protection of the bunkhouse. Once inside Andrea leaned against the door, trying to clear her blurred vision. It was a nightmare. She wanted desperately to sleep, to escape the terrible pounding and throbbing in her head.

She was startled back to the reality of the moment when she heard Stuart exclaim, 'Heather! Bruce! Thank God we've found you! But what are you doing here?' He knelt, his arms spreading with an almost imploring welcome. Andrea saw the children run to the kneeling figure, and knew Stuart was overcome with the relief of having found his children alive. He held them to his lean body with a fierceness that threatened to crush them, his face buried in their black curls.

Then like the changing of the wind, he lifted his face, relief submerged in a furious and violent anger. He pushed them from him and stood over them like a towering sentinel.

'And how did you two get here? What do you think you were doing going out in weather like this? Nothing short of stupidity could have taken you out in it in the first place. Do I have idiots for children? Answer me!' His words poured out, anger flushing his face, the pulse in his neck throbbing. 'You were born here, so you know what can happen. Have I taught you nothing?'

The children began to cry, terror glistening in their eyes. Stuart continued inexorably, uncaring about their fear and distress, 'You'll be severely punished for this. What you did wasn't just foolish and stupid, it was dangerous. You could have both died and we could have died looking for you!'

At this point Clayton moved towards him, speaking slowly and calmly, his hand resting on Stuart's arm in an attempt to restrain him. 'I found the kids, Stuart. They were pretty well shaken up when I got to them, and I'm sure they realise that what they did was both foolish and dangerous. They're still scared, Stuart, look at them. They don't need your anger now, they need reassurance.' Clayton spoke each word in an even steady voice.

Andrea broke in, supporting what Clayton had said, although understanding only too well how anger had been a natural reaction after the excruciating worry Stuart had been feeling. 'He's right, Stuart—they've been frightened enough. They've learned a lesson from this.'

Stuart turned on her, bitterly reminding her of her own words to him. 'They're *my* children, Andrea ... my children, and my responsibility. I will deal with this situation in the way I consider necessary.' His anger seemingly undiminished he pushed the twins towards the door. 'And now we'll go back to the house.'

Andrea noticed Clayton looking at Stuart and thought

she viewed an almost imperceptible shaking of his head. 'Don't you think we should wait until the storm is over, Stuart?' she asked.

He gave her a devastating look. 'The children and I are going back to the main house now. You can stay here if you like.' Turning to Clayton, he added, 'Let's get the chains on your jeep. We'll pull mine out when the storm's over.'

As Andrea refused to abandon the children to Stuart's wrath, she too climbed in the jeep. Somehow they managed to make it back to the house. Heather and Bruce clung tensely to Andrea all the way home. After they arrived, Stuart sent the twins upstairs to have a hot bath, but when Andrea started to follow them, she was prevented by the cold steel of Stuart's voice. 'No, they can do it themselves. Maybe you would be so kind as to get us all something hot to eat.' He turned to the large fireplace, knelt and began to build a fire. Andrea didn't bother to respond, but walked stiffly to the kitchen. She was cold and shaken and her head throbbed unceasingly. She pressed her hands to her eyes in an attempt to stop the pain.

'What's wrong?' Stuart demanded from behind her. She had not heard him come into the kitchen, and whirled in startled surprise. But she had turned too quickly, for his face slowly lost focus, melting in a blackness that was enveloping her entire body. She reached out, grasping at thin air. In a single movement he was beside her, holding her close to his strong body. She weakly pushed at him, mumbling, 'Let me go . . . I can't . . . You can't . . .' but she could neither continue nor fight his overpowering strength. He lifted her gently in his arms, walked quietly and carefully through the living-room, and up the stairs to her bedroom. Her face rested against his shoulder, like a child comforted and protected.

He softly placed her on the bed. 'Don't move, I'll get a cold cloth.'

'Oh no . . . not cold . . . I'm so cold now . . .' she muttered almost incoherently. In a few minutes he returned, placing a damp cloth over her eyes, one hand stroking her thick hair. As his gentle fingers soothed her forehead, he inadvertently touched the spot where she had struck her head. She flinched, drawing her breath in sharply.

'What is it? Are you hurt?' he questioned, his fingers pushed aside her hair, to reveal an already purpling welt. 'Andrea, you struck your head when the jeep went off the road, didn't you? Why didn't you tell me the truth when I asked you if you were hurt?' She looked fearfully at him, expecting to see another flash of anger, but there seemed to be none.

She replied, 'You had enough to worry about,' and continued, 'I'm all right, really. I feel better now . . . now that I'm lying down. Maybe I could just rest for a while.'

'I don't think you should sleep just yet, not so soon after striking your head,' he said, his eyes worried.

She looked at him. Yes, his eyes were worried and there was something else in them too, although she couldn't comprehend what. But there was no anger . . . the children would be all right with him now. And for the present, the tension was gone too. Her body relaxed. 'Just leave me for a while. I just want to rest, to be quiet. Just for a little while . . . please.'

He drew the comforter around her, looked down on her for what seemed a very long moment, and then silently left the room. She was asleep before the door clicked shut.

Stuart checked on Andrea often during the day and early evening, observing how her restless sleep gradually became more relaxed and easy. When he was not with her, he was downstairs with the children, sitting before the huge fire, watching them play or at times holding them close when they crawled up on to his lap. They had made their peace. Perhaps the shock of Andrea's collapse had wiped out his anger; not only had he made peace with his children, but somehow the pain and hurt with which he had been living for the past eight years had been eased, and now lay dormant within him . . . for a time at least.

Outside, the storm continued for most of the day, dying down at dusk. Clouds scudded over the mountains, revealing here and there a few stars, and the moon pushed through; together they were bright promises of a fine tomorrow.

It was the silence that finally awakened Andrea. She had floated back and forth between consciousness and sleep, in the beginning feeling stiff and uncomfortable, but after a while relaxing into a warm physical sensation of total peace and calm. She realised that the pain in her head had also gone. Slipping out of her slacks and into her night-dress, Andrea moved slowly from the bed to the window. It was dark. What time was it now? she wondered. How many hours had she slept? Were the children in bed? Outside, the whole world was soft and silent, like a sleeping child wrapped in a blanket of white wool. A light snow drifted gently and lazily to the quiet earth. The trees and fields glistened in the silver light of the full moon. The only sound was a gentle wind, the quiet breath of a sleeping white world.

Suddenly, cutting like a knife through the peace and solitude of the night, came the screaming of a child.

'Oh no! No! No! I don't want to be locked in. Please don't lock me in. I want to get out. Please don't leave me alone in here . . .' words rushing and crying, terror pulsing in the child's strained voice. It was Heather.

Not pausing a minute, Andrea rushed down the hall to the little girl's room. The door was closed, but not locked. Opening it quickly, Andrea saw the small figure sitting upright in the middle of the bed, almost as if she were in a trance, tears streaming down her white face. Andrea picked her up, held her close, and walked with her around the room, back and forth, attempting to soothe the frightened child, so small and helpless in her arms. 'Hush, baby, nothing's going to hurt you. Andrea's got you now. Hush . . . that's my girl . . .' Murmurings, over and over again in the stark quietness of the house.

Heather clung to her, gradually relaxing the strength of her grip around Andrea's neck. Her eyes were closed.

'Please, Barbara,' she whimpered, 'please, Barbara, don't lock the door. Don't lock me in again. I promise . . .' her small voice trailed off . . . 'I promise I won't . . .'

In that moment Andrea turned to see Stuart standing in the doorway, the light from the hall shining on his pale, exhausted face, his hand raised against the doorframe, as if for support. She started to move towards him, but he raised his hand and shaking his head, motioned to her to stay with Heather until she slept. When Andrea looked again he had gone.

Heather finally slept. Andrea lowered the child back in her bed, standing by her for a few minutes to make certain that she was asleep, then she tiptoed from the room, leaving the light on in the hallway in case Heather reawakened. On the way back to her own room, Andrea saw a light shining under Stuart's door. Without stopping to think, inwardly astonished by her boldness, she quietly opened the door to see Stuart sitting in a chair near the window, his head leaning forward, resting on his hands. He turned to her, his face lined and drawn, his eyes pained, so that her heart ached at the sight of him. She walked towards him.

'Oh God, Andrea,' he whispered, 'I thought it was over. For them, at least, I thought it was over.'

'I'm sorry, I don't understand, Stuart,' Andrea breathed softly, frightened that a louder voice would cause him to withdraw.

His hand reached for hers. He held it lightly, moving his fingers back and forth over the creamy smoothness of her skin.

'I wanted to tell you . . . before. I wanted to share it with you. But somehow, I couldn't . . .'

'It's about Barbara, isn't it, Stuart?' Andrea offered. 'It has something to do with your dead wife Barbara, hasn't it?'

'Yes, it has everything to do with my dead wife Barbara.' He spoke every word succinctly and with a profound bitterness.

Andrea spoke gently. 'Don't you think it's about time that *you* laid a ghost to rest, Stuart?'

He looked up at her and, breathing a heavy sigh, muttered, 'Yes, I suppose it is time I did that, Andrea. But it's a long and difficult story for me to tell.' He paused, then began slowly, 'I started writing when I was in my early twenties. When I was twenty-five I wrote my first play. Fortunately, or perhaps unfortunately ... I'm not sure which sometimes ... it was an instant success, an instant huge success. It was being produced in New York, and I went there to live for a while. That's when I met Barbara; she was one of the actresses in my play. She was well known, talented and beautiful. I was a young and promising writer with a bright future in the theatre. We first met at a party and four months later, we married. I thought at the time it was love—although infatuation was more like it. Anyway, it was short-lived and the most destructive thing I've ever experienced. The honeymoon barely lasted a week. I wanted to live in Alberta, and raise a family there. I couldn't see living in New York—I just wouldn't fit. We'd talked this over before we married, and Barbara had agreed totally with my views, but as soon as we came here to live, it was a different matter, and the marriage was as good as over. She seemed to try for a few days, then became possessed with hating the place and me with it. We began to argue, not only over that, but also about having children. Barbara had changed her mind about that, too. She said she couldn't stand to be tied down by babies or to lose her good looks and figure for nine months.

'Then we discovered she was pregnant. It was ironic really that we had twins, two babies when Barbara hated the very idea of even having one child. After she gave birth to Heather and Bruce, that was it; our marriage became a marriage in name only. Barbara went her way, I went mine. She spent some of her time here, with many trips to New York. When she was here, she lived in her own section of the house. She often entertained there ... she always had an unlimited supply of male admirers.' Anger suffused his voice again. 'It was one affair after another. I tried to discuss divorce, but she would have none of it; for some sadistic reason, she somehow preferred our arrangement.' His face muscles tightened, 'Sometimes I think I could have come close to killing her, I so wanted to be free of the pain and the disgrace she brought to this house.'

'But what about the children? Didn't Barbara care for them?' Andrea asked, appalled by this stark recital.

He shook his head. 'Barbara cared for no one but Barbara. Sometimes she would make a show of being "mother" for her friends, but it was always an act of which she tired quickly. Basically, Maggie brought up the children.'

He looked very weary, and now the words came slowly. Andrea sat down on the floor at his feet, putting his hand to her mouth, moving her lips over the tanned skin of his long fingers. He went on, 'That's what Heather's nightmare is about. Barbara would lock the children in their rooms when she wanted them out of her way, which was often. I wasn't always here, so it was a while before I knew what was happening. When I did find out, we had one hell of a row, but she wouldn't listen to me about anything by this time. How she hated me! I offered her her freedom and I begged for mine, but she wouldn't agree. She said that she liked the arrangement just fine.'

His eyes narrowed in the half light of the room. 'I had grounds for divorce, because she took no pains to hide her affairs—in fact, she openly flaunted them in my face. But during the last big argument we had, she swore that she would take the children if I pushed it and she would make sure I would never see them again.'

He closed his eyes, his voice choked with emotion. 'I couldn't let them go, Andrea, no matter what she did to me I couldn't let them go. They were all that I loved, and she would destroy them too if she took them. I stayed away from her as much as I could, although it was impossible at times, but I tried. Sometimes I thought I couldn't live with this insanity one second longer ... but I did. For the children's sake I continued with our bizarre marriage. The ultimate irony was that she did finally decide to leave me, and two weeks later was killed in a car accident with the man who was her latest diversion. That was four years ago. Heather was left with her nightmares, although they're less frequent now, and I was left with my own kind of nightmare. I awaken sometimes at night in a cold sweat, thinking that Barbara is still here. She's reaching out to strangle me and ... all that I love. Even now, years later, she haunts me, and it's not always a nightmare which needs the night to reappear. I want it to end, Andrea,' he muttered wearily. 'How much and how long must a man pay for one mistake? She came very close to destroying me ... so very close ... and I feel sometimes that she still may do it. I know that doesn't sound rational, but it's the feeling that I have ... her ghost won't rest.'

He stared down at the girl at his feet, whose burnished hair was spread across his thigh, and whose slim fingers were intertwined with his. Slowly she raised her eyes; they were brimming with tears. 'Don't cry, my dear,' he pleaded.

'Oh, Stuart, what a dreadful story! I'm so sorry for all the pain you've been through.' Almost unconscious of what she was doing, she brought his hand up to her lips again; a tear dripped on his palm. 'Have you ever told anyone about it before?'

'No, never. How could I share something like that?'

'Then perhaps just sharing it will help to banish Barbara's ghost,' she suggested hopefully, feeling an unbidden thrill of pleasure that it was in her that he had finally confided.

He smiled, a smile that erased the lines of strain around his mouth, even as his eyes kindled with sudden warmth. Abruptly Andrea became aware of the lateness of the hour, and of the fact that she was clad only in a flimsy night-gown, while Stuart was wearing silk pyjamas, the jacket unbuttoned to the waist. Rosy colour flooded her cheeks and she moved away from him uncertainly.

His hands slid down her arms to her elbows, and he stood up, raising her to her feet as well. A new strength infused his voice. 'I know how to lay the past to rest, Andrea.'

'How?' she whispered, searching his serious face with her deep brown eyes.

'You can do it for me.'

'I?' she breathed.

'Yes, you. Dearest Andrea, I want you so much. I've wanted you since I first saw you lost and alone in the snow. You're so young and so innocent ... and so very lovely. Look at you now—your eyes are shining like stars. Can that mean that you love me too?'

She gave an incredulous, breathless laugh. 'But you haven't said you love me, yet!'

He threw back his head and laughed out loud. 'The famous playwright is botching his love scene, sweetheart!' Abruptly he sobered. His grey eyes intent on her face, he said with deep seriousness, 'I love you, Andrea. More than life itself, I love you.'

Her heart pounded with boundless joy. Stuart loved her ... so her love for him was not the solitary and fruitless passion she had believed it to be. She looked tenderly into the dark depths of his eyes. 'Oh Stuart, I love you too. I love you so much I've thought my heart would break with the ache of it.' She lowered her gaze, her lashes dark shadows against her cheeks. 'I never dreamed you would ... could ... love me.'

His arms enfolded her, drawing her close to the warmth of his big body. 'I want to marry you, Andrea ... right away, if you'll have me.'

'Yes, I will marry you,' she replied, joy resounding in her voice.

'This week?'

'Tomorrow!' she said recklessly.

Again laughter shook him. 'I'm afraid there are formalities like licences and things to deal with.' Possessively his eyes roamed over her tumbled hair, her flushed cheeks, the throbbing pulse at the base of her slender neck. With one finger he traced the line of her collarbone, his hand brushing the soft swell of her breast. She shivered with delight, her body unconsciously swaying towards him.

His lips found hers in a kiss of deepening passion. With every fibre of her being she was aware of his impatient hands caressing her body, smoothing the curves of her waist and hips. Her lips parted under his. Drowning in desire, she was distantly aware of the thudding of his heart against her palm, of his harsh breathing.

Finally he freed her mouth, and for a long moment they looked into each other's eyes. 'Sweetheart, sweetheart,' he murmured, 'I want you, I want you now. But we'll be married in a week, and then we'll be lovers in every sense of the word.'

They clung to each other for a long time, while the tumultuous emotions each had experienced slowly subsided into a peace and contentment that was just as meaningful. Together, Andrea thought, they would build a new life, sharing all the things this life would bring ... children, laughter, joy, and love. No ghost of the past would be able to waken Stuart's nightmare to reality, for together they would put the past to rest.

CHAPTER FIVE

IT was Andrea's wedding day.

Waking early, she lay still for a few minutes, warm and relaxed in the comfortable cocoon of her sheets and blankets. Happiness awakened with her, awakened and expanded until she was pervaded with it ... her wedding day! Today she would marry Stuart, become his wife; shyly she regarded the wide expanse of her bed, knowing that tonight she would not sleep alone. Her lips curved involuntarily as she lovingly recalled his lean body, his imperious hands, and searching kisses. Until now, he had restrained his ardour, for, like herself, he believed in the sanctity of the marriage vows.

Her face clouded temporarily as she remembered how cruelly those vows had been desecrated by Barbara—such disillusionment would never recur, Andrea promised herself with silent wholeheartedness; she would devote herself, body and soul, to Stuart Trent, to fulfilling him as Barbara had not, to giving him the love and warmth—and reassurance—he needed. It was odd to think of a word like reassurance in connection with Stuart's strength and masculinity, but deep within her she knew he still had scars to heal, raw wounds left by Barbara's callous and careless handling. Oh God, she prayed fervently, let me love him as he should be loved ... may we always be happy together ... yet how foolish she was being to even imagine things could ever be otherwise!

However, the previous week had not been without its bad moments, most of the conflict being directly traceable to Cynthia. Andrea sighed. She and Stuart had both agreed that her aunt should be invited to the wedding, but neither of them had anticipated she would take the first plane to Calgary and stay with them for the entire week before the wedding. Their one desire had been to spend as much time as

possible alone together, to marvel anew over the incredible
wonder of their love, but everywhere they turned they had
tripped over Cynthia, her strident voice interrupting their
low-voiced conversations, her clumsy attempts at discipline
upsetting the children. And yesterday, six days after she
had arrived, had provided the climax to the week. Andrea
could remember exactly how it had happened . . .

Cynthia had found Andrea eating breakfast by herself, as
Stuart had already left for the ranch. 'Good morning, dear!
Don't tell me you're alone! How nice, we can have a cosy
chat.'

Andrea's appetite deserted her in a flash, since there was
nothing particularly 'nice' in the prospect of a cosy chat
with her aunt. But trying to be civil, for she was all the
family Cynthia had, she said, 'Can I get you a grapefruit?
You always liked those for breakfast, didn't you?'

'Thank you, dear. You look tired this morning, you must
have been up late last night, were you?'

Andrea coloured. She and Stuart had been late; they had
sat talking and dreaming in front of the fire in the study, he
in the armchair, she leaning against his knees, his fingers
playing with the heavy strands of her hair. But she did not
feel like sharing the peace and seclusion of that experience
with her aunt. 'It wasn't that late,' she evaded. 'Anyway,
I'm twenty-two years old, and should surely be allowed up
after midnight,' she added in a show of defiance.

'Yes, you are twenty-two, aren't you? I think I've been
guilty of underestimating you, Andrea; I suppose I still
think of you as sixteen. But here you've managed to snare
the famous Simon Ward, and that's no mean accomplishment. How long have you actually known him?'

'Only a month. But time has very little to do with it,'
Andrea said indignantly, thinking what a dreaful word
'snare' was to use in connection with her and Stuart.

'You're obviously a fast worker,' her aunt said in ap-
proval.

Andrea grimaced. She and Cynthia had rarely seen eye to
eye on anything, their value systems being entirely different, but perhaps it was worth trying to clarify the situa-

tion. 'I love him,' she said with gentle dignity. 'And he loves me. It's that simple.'

Cynthia's tinkle of laughter grated on her niece's ears as much as it ever had. 'Hardly that simple, you silly child. There's the little matter of a great deal of money thrown in. He's a very rich man, as even you must be aware. What allowance does he intend to give you, and what provision has he made for you in his will?'

'I have no idea!' Andrea exploded, horrified by this mercenary attitude. 'We've never discussed money. Anyway, I'd marry him if he was a pauper.'

'But how very pleasant that he's not,' her aunt said cynically. 'Well, I really must congratulate you, Andrea, you've played your cards very well. However, as your only relative, I feel I should give you a word or two of warning and advice.'

Gritting her teeth, Andrea sat back in her chair, knowing nothing would stop Cynthia now.

'Stuart is so much older than you, dear, and so much more worldly-wise. I can see why your air of innocence appeals to him, but you'll need more than innocence to hold a man like him. Don't forget he's not just Stuart Trent, he's also Simon Ward, and as such is at home in a very different milieu from this backwoods type of existence. What do you have to offer him that can compare?' With total insensitivity, she added, 'Your skating career?'

Andrea winced. 'Stuart knows all about that,' she said hotly.

'He knows about your knee injury?'

'It hardly troubles me at all now.'

Abandoning this line of attack, Cynthia probed further. 'And what about Ronald? Does Stuart know about him?'

In utter consternation Andrea stared at her aunt. 'Ronald?' she faltered.

'Why, yes—Ronald Martin. There was a letter from his mother waiting for me when I got back from Europe.'

'It was full of lies,' Andrea said vehemently.

'My dear, I haven't told you what it said yet.'

'Since you're obviously dying to tell me about it, you might as well go ahead.'

'Of course, I don't know when you met Stuart. But it would appear to be only a short time after you tried—unsuccessfully, I presume—to seduce Ronald Martin.'

Even though Andrea had been more or less prepared for this, she still felt helpless anger well up inside her. She kept a firm grip on her temper, because she was determined to clear up the misunderstanding for once and for all. 'I did not try to seduce him,' she said, speaking as slowly and clearly as if she were addressing a backward child. 'The situation was quite the reverse. He wouldn't leave me alone.' Even in retrospect, she shuddered. 'He revolted me, if you want the truth.'

'Come now, Andrea,' her aunt chided, 'he's a presentable and wealthy young man, although not nearly as rich as Stuart, of course. You don't have to feel ashamed for trying to attract his attention. I'm sure you weren't the first girl to do so.'

'I didn't try to attract his attention! I loathed him, and I hope I never set eyes on him again!'

Cynthia's gaze sharpened. 'The chances are quite good that you'll meet him again. Aren't you aware that Stuart knows the Martins?'

'No . . . I had no idea of that.' Stunned, Andrea gazed at her aunt.

'Ronald has a startlingly beautiful older sister, Cecile, whom Stuart squired around Vancouver and New York for quite some time. In fact, I think everyone, including Cecile herself, thought they would marry eventually.'

Just to hear Stuart's name juxtaposed with that of another woman sent a scorching flash of jealousy through Andrea's body. In a general way she had recognised that he must have known other women in the months and years since Barbara had died, but it was a different matter to hear a specific name, particularly when it was the sister of the loathsome Ronald. Cecile . . . and she was beautiful . . .

'You'd better be careful how you handle this, dear.' Cynthia's voice broke into her reverie. 'You were wise to

insist on a small wedding, because otherwise the Martins
would undoubtedly have been invited.'

'Neither of us wanted a big society wedding,' Andrea
protested. 'It was nothing to do with the Martins. I just
finished telling you, I didn't even realise Stuart knew they
existed.'

'Well, now you do. It's a very delicate situation. As far as
I know, Stuart liked Ronald; he certainly liked Cecile. I
don't think he'll be particularly pleased to discover you had
Ronald in your bedroom only a few weeks ago.'

Andrea gave a sigh of total frustration and gathering
tension. Cynthia was plainly convinced that her niece had
attempted to seduce Ronald for his money, had failed, and
had moved on, more successfully, to bigger game. 'I'll tell
Stuart the truth about the whole thing,' she said. 'He was
deceived by his first wife, but he won't be by his second.'

'That would be a very foolish move,' said Cynthia incisively, 'particularly now, with the wedding tomorrow. If
you feel you must tell him something, wait until you're
married, and the children are back in school, and you can
pick your time. Cecile is in the Bahamas, so it's unlikely
you'll meet her in the near future.'

Andrea chewed on her lip indecisively, deeply regretting
that she had not told Stuart the truth about her short stay
with the Martins when they had first met; it would have
been much simpler. The very fact that she had concealed
the story from him put her in a bad light. He would believe
her, of course, for he was not like Cynthia. But perhaps the
latter was right—she should wait until after the wedding.
She knew Stuart was harassed and tired; in order to take a
few days off for their honeymoon, he was trying to complete his work on the play and also to deal with certain
financial matters concerning the ranch. She would tell him
in a few days, not now when he was so pressured by business.

He came home for lunch, weary and sweat-stained in an
old checked shirt and faded denim jeans. When he entered
the room, his eyes immediately sought Andrea's, the glow
of love in them kindling an answering fire in hers. He put

his hands on her shoulders and kissed her. 'I won't get any closer,' he murmured, lines of laughter deepening in his cheeks. 'I'm filthy.'

She rubbed her nose against his shirt front. 'It's called what your best friend won't tell you,' she chuckled, then suddenly flung her arms around his waist, burying her face in his shoulder, a catch in her voice. 'Oh, Stuart, I do love you.'

'Hey,' he said quietly, 'what brought that on? Are you okay?'

She nodded, not wanting to meet his eyes, and wishing she and Cynthia had not had that conversation, for now Ronald seemed to be sneering at them over her shoulder. And why had Stuart never mentioned his relationship with Cecile? Honesty was a two-way street, wasn't it?

With these thoughts swirling in her brain, she wasn't surprised when Stuart gently pushed her away and looked down at her, his grey eyes shrewd and penetrating. 'What's the matter? Last-minute doubts before you go to the altar?'

'Heavens, no!' she exclaimed, her wide-eyed astonishment at such a thought making her laugh. She squared her shoulders—she would explain the whole sorry story about the Martins, and put her trust in him. She opened her mouth, only to have Cynthia's coy voice interject, 'Here you both are! Oh dear, have I interrupted a lovers' tiff?'

'No,' said Stuart, as near to rudeness as his good manners would allow, 'we scarcely have time for a tiff, even if we wanted one.'

Impervious to the implied criticism, Cynthia continued blithely, 'Well then, Andrea dear, I do hope you're insisting on finding out more about your future financial position. She's such a ninny, Stuart, she's never had any idea about the value of money.'

'Oddly enough, I find that one of Andrea's virtues,' Stuart replied grimly. 'It's nice to be valued for myself for a change, and not for my possessions.'

The older woman looked decidedly put out. 'I have to disagree with you. Andrea needs a thorough education in the handling of money. How would she ever have got as far as she did with her figure skating if I hadn't looked after her finances? Not that she ever did make it to the top.'

'That was scarcely her fault!' Stuart exclaimed, finally goaded out of his usual courtesy. 'And as for the money, I gather Andrea has been paying you back ever since. At least you can't accuse her of a lack of indebtedness.'

Although Andrea was partly distressed by this quarrel, she could not help feeling both gratified and proud that Stuart had sprung so quickly to her defence.

Two ugly patches of colour stained Cynthia's heavily powdered cheeks. 'I hope you will never be disappointed in my niece, Stuart; it's a dangerous thing to put someone on a pedestal.'

'To have a true appreciation of someone's worth is not necessarily putting them on a pedestal. I trust Andrea, and I love her for her honesty and innocence. Even her chastity, to use a thoroughly old-fashioned word.'

Defeated, Cynthia gave Andrea one last meaningful glance before she left the room. 'You'd better remember my advice, hadn't you, my dear?' was her parting shot.

Andrea was saved the trouble of a reply by the precipitate arrival of the twins, both bursting to describe their latest explorations on the ranch. As Stuart dealt with their garbled explanations, the watching girl came to the inescapable conclusion that she could not broach the subject of Ronald now. With Stuart's words about her honesty ringing in her ears, how could she tell him that she had been less than honest with him about her previous employers? Much as she hated to do it, she would have to take Cynthia's advice and delay her explanations . . .

There was a surreptitious tap at the bedroom door. 'Are you awake, Andrea?' a little voice enquired.

'Yes, I am. Come in.'

Heather edged around the door. 'Daddy said I wasn't to wake you up. Maggie's going to bring your breakfast up here, because you mustn't see Daddy until you get married. So he's going to the ranch after breakfast. Why can't you see him, Andrea?'

'It's supposed to bring bad luck.'

'Oh. Can I help you get dressed this afternoon? The sun's shining, so you'll be able to get married outdoors like you wanted to.'

'Of course you can. Once I've had my breakfast, we'll get everything out—your clothes too.'

Andrea passed the morning in a trance-like state of joyous expectation; even Cynthia came to her with a stiffly worded apology for her behaviour of the day before, and far too happy to hold a grudge, Andrea embraced her forgivingly. After lunch she helped Heather into her long pink dress, tied her sash, and brushed her black curls, arranging a circlet of tiny rosebuds in her hair. Then she put on her own gown. It was pure white, at Stuart's request, fashioned of a heavy satin which emphasised the femininity of her tiny waist and high bosom. Picking up a spray of feathery white orchids, she smiled at the little girl and said softly, 'Let's go. Oh, darling, I'm so happy!'

They walked down the stairs together, where Bruce, Cynthia, Maggie and Clayton were waiting, Clayton almost unrecognisably smart in a suit, white shirt and figured tie, Maggie regal in puce brocade with a matching hat, and a corsage of tawny roses. Because of their unfamiliar appearance, Andrea was abruptly seized by the traditional prenuptial nervousness; four weeks ago she had not even known Stuart and now she was to marry him ... what did they know about each other? How could they have contemplated such a momentous step after the brevity and storminess of their acquaintance?

'Calm down,' said Clayton soothingly, patting her as though she were a flighty colt. 'It's only stage fright. The groom's twice as scared as you, so let's not keep the poor man waiting any longer, eh?'

Her smile broke through. 'Is he really?'

'Nervous as a kitten, shaking like a leaf.'

And because it was so ridiculous to think of Stuart shaking like a leaf, Andrea was still smiling as she walked out of the front door into the spring sunlight, her hand resting on Clayton's sleeve.

It was unseasonably warm. The grass was already misted with new green, unfurling buds danced on the poplars, and the spruce grove echoed with the melodious ripple of a thrush's song. It seemed unbelievable to Andrea that just a little over a week ago they had been in the midst of a raging blizzard. Warm chinook winds, accompanied by a dramatic rise in temperature, had melted the snow within a few days, until now no evidence of the storm's fury could be found. Stuart was standing on the lawn with the clergyman who was to marry them, his long body silhouetted against a backdrop of fields, trees, and the jagged teeth of the distant Rockies. He looked frighteningly formal in a tailored morning suit, and as she walked across the grass with his two children on either side of her, she was again attacked by unreasoning panic.

But then he turned towards her, his dark eyes grave and steady on the haunting beauty of her face, framed by a fragile lace veil. Hypnotised by his gaze, she moved to his side, knowing it was the place where she belonged—for ever. The marriage ceremony began, and as she pledged herself to him, she was awed by the intense love naked in Stuart's eyes for all to see. She had no way of foreseeing how soon that love would be put to the test.

The next few hours passed in a blur of enchantment. Caterers had prepared a delicious buffet supper for the wedding party, during which Stuart toasted his new bride in champagne. Bruce was unimpressed by his first taste of caviare, and Cynthia unbent sufficiently to kiss her niece's husband on the cheek. Afterwards Andrea changed into a spring suit of palest turquoise with a ruffled blouse of flowered chiffon, and managed to persuade a reluctant Heather to exchange the pink dress for her school clothes. In Stuart's Mercedes they drove to Calgary, first taking the children back to school.

' 'Bye, Andrea,' Heather whispered, hugging her closely. 'You're my new mother now, aren't you?'

'Yes, darling, and just as soon as this last term's over, you'll be living at home all the time—and don't forget we'll be seeing you both next weekend.' She bent to kiss Bruce

and abruptly he too flung his arms around her neck in a
boyish stranglehold. Her vision obscured by a mist of tears,
Andrea watched them disappear into the dormitory.

'You're going to make a wonderful mother, sweetheart,'
Stuart said huskily. 'For Heather and Bruce—and for our
own children.'

Blushing rosily, she teased, 'After we take Cynthia to the
airport, perhaps we can discuss that subject!'

'Only married four hours, and you're ordering me around
already!' he groaned.

At the airport Cynthia boarded the jet to Halifax. Then,
ignoring the jostling crowds, Stuart took his wife in his
arms. 'Kiss me,' he ordered.

Laughingly she glanced around at the milling travellers.
'Here?'

'They'll think you've just flown in from Timbuctoo and I
haven't seen you for six months.'

'I don't think I promised to obey, did I?'

He seized her in a hard embrace, stifling her laughing
protests with his lips. Then he murmured, 'Although I hate
to admit it, you're right—there are too many people here. I
think it's time we began our honeymoon, Mrs Trent. And
for that, we need to be alone.'

Stuart had kept their destination a surprise to Andrea;
he had rented a luxurious chalet in the mountains its
privacy ensured by the acres of forest that surrounded it.
When they arrived, he went ahead to unlock the door.

Andrea waited by the car, listening to the rustle and sigh
of the wind in the tree branches; an owl hooted, its waver-
ing cry eerie in the pitch darkness. She shivered, knowing
that her palms were damp and her heart was fluttering
against her rib cage. It was silly to be afraid of being alone
with her beloved Stuart, but afraid she was. For the first
time in her life she wished she were less innocent, more
experienced . . .

Stuart walked back towards her, a giant of a man, a
demanding and ardent man who was now her lawfully
wedded husband and who would soon demand from her the
consummation of their love. She stood rooted to the spot,

backed defensively against the car. Apparently unaware of her fear, he swung her up into his arms. 'Tradition demands I carry my bride across the threshold,' he said gallantly, carrying her into the chalet and putting her down in the lounge. It was a spacious slant-ceilinged room, panelled in knotty pine and centred by an immense granite fireplace. 'There's a fireplace in our room too,' he commented casually. 'I'll start the fire in there. Do you want to put the kettle on? The kitchen's through there.'

The prosaic nature of his request reassured her somewhat, although as she washed her hands in the sink, she knew they were icy-cold to the touch. She prepared coffee and carried the steaming mugs through into the lounge. 'Bring it here, would you?' Stuart called from the bedroom. 'The wood was a bit damp, so I want to keep an eye on it.'

He was kneeling by the hearth, feeding sticks of kindling to the crackling flames. Absently he brushed his hands down his trousers and accepted the coffee from her. Grateful that she was being ignored, she surveyed the room. The walls were stuccoed, while the sliding glass doors led out on to a patio that in the daylight must command a magnificent view of the mountain peaks. She took off her shoes and wriggled her toes in the ivory shag carpet, unable any longer to disregard the vast bed that dominated the room.

'I brought your case in, why don't you change into something more comfortable?' said Stuart, taking a sip of his coffee and putting another log on the fire.

Mutely she did as she was told. The bathroom, attractively decorated in shades of blue and green, was completely modern and immaculately clean. She showered, hoping in vain that the spray of hot water would relax her overstretched nerves, then put on the white tricot negligée that had seemed so entirely right when she had tried it on in the shop last week, but which now seemed almost indecently transparent, revealing far more of herself than it should. She dragged a brush through her hair, procrastinating her return to the bedroom.

'Andrea? Are you all right? Can I come and wash my

hands?' Apparently construing her silence for consent, he pushed open the door, and stared in concern at his wife's face, as paper-white as her ruffled robe. 'Sweetheart! What's wrong?'

'I'm scared,' she quavered, too frightened to prevaricate.

'Of me?' he said incredulously.

She nodded, looking down at her clenched fingers in order to avoid his discerning eyes. He had taken off his jacket and had unbuttoned his shirt, pulling it out of the waistband of his trousers; there was dark matted hair on his bare chest and on the muscles of his forearms. 'It's all right for you,' she said, hopelessly tactless. 'You've—slept with someone before. I never have.'

'I know you haven't, you silly goose.' Swiftly he enfolded her tense form in his arms. 'I'm sorry, love, I should have realised . . . please don't be frightened. I'll be as gentle with you as I can. And now, come in by the fire, you're freezing.'

He guided her back into the bedroom, where he sat in the big armchair beside the fireplace, pulling her down on his lap. He stroked her shoulder with one hand, and with the other played with her cold fingers. 'Remember how we met?' he began. 'I'll never forget how you materialised out of the blizzard, like a lost spirit of the forest . . .' his voice quiet, his hands infinitely soothing, he reminisced in the same vein, until imperceptibly her limbs warmed and with a sigh of surrender she relaxed against his hard chest. His lips moved to her hair, inhaling its dusky fragrance, then down the softness of her cheek, and finally found her mouth.

Deep within her all resistance melted, overcome by his patience and tenderness. Tentatively her lips moved under his kiss; she could feel his heartbeat quicken through the thin fabric of her negligée. His mouth grew more demanding, his hand slid from her shoulder to the softness of her breast; she quivered with delight, her own hands pushing aside his shirt to caress the muscular hardness of his torso. Aching with the desire to become one with him, she moaned his name, scarcely aware that the straps of her nightgown had slipped to her waist, her fingers tangled in the thick curls of his hair as he buried his face in the scented valley between her breasts. No longer able to restrain himself, he picked her up and carried her to the bed ...

Some time in the middle of the night Andrea awoke. She felt momentarily disorientated, until beside her she heard the quiet breathing of her husband. An involuntary smile tugged at her lips. Stuart ... her husband, whose long body was lying against hers, one arm heavy against her breast. She lay motionless, not wanting to disturb him, recalling with what tenderness and care he had made love to her such a short time ago. A little sigh of sheer happiness escaped her.

'Awake, my love?' his voice said through the darkness.

'Mmm ... and thinking about you.'

'What were you thinking?' he murmured drowsily.

'I can't tell you,' she teased. 'It would be very bad for your ego.' She squealed as he ran a finger along the length of her spine.

'I'll tickle you until you tell me,' he threatened.

Giggling, she gave in. 'I was thinking you're the nicest man I've ever known, and I love you very much.'

He nuzzled her ear with a lazy sensuality that made her heart flutter against her ribs. 'You expressed that beautifully,' he complimented her. 'And now come here, my lady wife, because I find I want you again.'

Willingly she obeyed, her own passion meeting his, and the world dissolved as they became one.

Three weeks later, Andrea was sitting on the fence of the ranch corral, watching the branding of the new heifers with mingled fascination and revulsion. From the herd crowded against the fence Stuart's horse singled out the next animal, which Stuart lassoed and threw to the ground. In one swift movement the man dismounted and knelt on the struggling calf, while Clayton pressed the red-hot iron against its flank. Andrea grimaced, recognising that the process was necessary, but hating the stench of singed hair and the bewildered bawling of the cattle.

By way of distraction she let her eyes linger on her husband, knowing she could do so without him noticing, since he was wrapped up in the task at hand. He was wearing tight-fitting levis over tooled leather boots, and a faded blue shirt that was far from clean. It hardly seemed possible they had been married for over three weeks, she marvelled; the days before the wedding seemed an aeon ago. With the growing pride and confidence of a woman well loved, she could look back on the fears of her wedding night with both incredulity and amusement; since then she had changed from a shy and innocent girl to a mature, contented woman. Physically and emotionally Stuart could meet her every need, and with an increasing sense of wonder she had discovered she could give him equal pleasure and fulfilment. He was a perfect lover, alternately passionate or tender ... even to think about him turned her bones to water.

They had spent nearly a week at the chalet, and then had brought the children home to the ranch for the weekend, a practice that had continued each weekend since then. They had become a family of four almost without noticing, so smoothly had it happened, for the children had accepted their father's marriage to Andrea with total ease and readiness. The intensity of Andrea's new-found happiness sometimes frightened her ... such perfection was surely more than she deserved. Sitting in the sun by the dust-filled corral, she closed her eyes, praying for it to last for ever.

She was roused from her reverie by someone calling her name, and she looked back towards the bunkhouse. One of the cowhands—Tom, or was it Pete?—was waving at her. She slid down from the fence and trotted across to him. 'Maggie just phoned. There was a long-distance call for Mr Trent from New York. He's to phone back as soon as possible.'

Without the slightest premonition of what this phone call was to mean to her, Andrea said, 'Thanks! I'll go and tell him now.'

At the corral gate she shouted above the din, 'Stuart!

Stuart!' He wheeled his buckskin gelding and cantered over to her, pushing back his stetson and wiping his forehead with the back of his hand. 'What's up, love?'

She relayed the message, letting her eyes wander possessively over his tanned features, from which sweat trickled to the hollow at the base of his throat. 'Keep looking at me like that,' he said in a low voice, for her ears alone, 'and I won't be answerable for the consequences . . . we'll end up in the bunkhouse.'

She let her thick hair fall coyly over her face. 'Whatever gave you the impression I was that kind of girl?'

'Last night, and the night before, and . . .'

'All right! All right! I get the message,' she responded, helpless with laughter.

Twin flames of devilment in his eyes, he guided the buckskin towards the fence and pulled her from her perch. She shrieked in mock alarm and grabbed him around the waist. 'Am I being abducted?' she giggled. Rubbing her cheek against the long line of his spine, she added, 'You're all dirty.'

'Nothing but complaints,' he answered amiably, then abruptly continued, 'Damn it, Andrea, I wonder who's trying to get in touch with me. You don't know how much I've enjoyed these past few days on the ranch. To hell with plays and New York!'

He dug his heels into the horse's sides, and in companionable silence they jogged down the trail to the house. Summer had come to the foothills, the grass green and lush in the ditches, the track overhung with leafy branches that dappled them with shadows. In the sky the swallows swooped and chirruped in their ceaseless search for insects. Afterwards Andrea was to remember this ride home as the last unsullied contentment she and Stuart were to share on the ranch for a long time . . . she had been right to fear for her happiness.

As her husband ran into the house in his anxiety to solve the mystery, she tethered the buckskin and slowly wandered after him, wondering at her reluctance. She wanted no outsiders in her paradise, she thought ruefully, not even long-distance ones. She could hear Stuart talking in the study, so she sat in a shaft of sunlight on one of the window seats in the hall to wait for him. She did not have long to wait. He came out of the study, raking his fingers through his disordered hair. 'Oh, there you are,' he said unceremoniously. 'I guess we'd better pack our suitcases.'

'Why, Stuart?'

'That was Milton Wallace, my New York producer. The new play is to be launched as soon as possible, so he wants me there for probably a month, if not longer. New York at this time of year—it'll be as hot as Hades!'

'Do you have to go?' she asked. 'Couldn't someone else do it?'

'Of course I have to go!' he snapped.

It had been many weeks since he had spoken to her like that. She flinched, realising suddenly how vulnerable her love for Stuart had made her.

He must have seen her involuntary movement. 'I'm sorry, darling,' he apologised. 'I'm as cross as a bear, but it's not your fault.' Holding her by the shoulders, he said seriously, 'I'm just about ready to give up writing plays. I don't want to go to New York—I want to stay here with you and the children. But I've committed myself, so I'll have to go this time. At least you can come with me—I'd better phone the airport and make reservations. Be sure you pack some of those pretty dresses you bought; undoubtedly we'll get dragged to innumerable cocktail parties.'

So relieved to have him smiling at her again that she would have done anything he asked, she said, 'Do you realise I've never been to a party with you before? And please will you take me to the Metropolitan Museum and to the top of the Empire State Building?'

'I'll take you anywhere your heart desires.' He kissed her quickly on the tip of her nose. 'I guess reality had to intrude sooner or later, didn't it?'

'I'm afraid I don't want to share you with anyone else,' she replied, knowing it was a foolish sentiment, yet wanting to tell him anyway.

'The feeling's mutual. But we'll get lots of time together, so don't worry.'

Early the following evening they had arrived in New York and Stuart was unlocking the door of his penthouse apartment on Park Avenue. 'The caretaker cleaned and aired it today, and laid in a stock of food, so we should be okay,' he said. 'We'd better hurry if we're going to make it to the restaurant in time.'

Even his voice sounded tired, Andrea thought with concern, noting the pallor beneath his tan and the deepened lines in his forehead. 'Why don't you have a shower and then make me a cocktail—a Manhattan would be appropriate!—while I investigate the kitchen,' she said. 'I'm sure I can make an omelette, or something like that. I really don't feel like battling with the traffic and the noise and all those people again today.'

'But, Andrea, I promised you dinner at Maxim's our first night in New York.'

'You're not getting out of it altogether,' she laughed. 'You can take me tomorrow.'

'You're an angel,' he said feelingly. 'An omelette sounds wonderful. Did I tell you today I love you?'

She cocked her head on one side. 'Only three times, I think. You're slipping!' She gave him a little push. 'Go and have your shower,' she ordered, filled with pleasure that she had handled a potentially tense situation correctly.

She slept late the next morning, long after Stuart had gone to the theatre, and in the afternoon ventured out into the city for a hair appointment; the first of the cocktail parties was that very evening. The hairdresser gathered her heavy dark hair into a smooth coronet on her head, leaving curled tendrils to fall softly about her ears. When Stuart finally arrived back at the apartment, she was making up her face in front of the mirror, clad only in her nylon undies and a lacy slip. He came up behind her, and she tilted her face to smile at his reflection. Oh dear, she thought, he did look tired again . . . his hands slid sensually across her bare shoulders to cup her breasts, and he laid his cheek against her neck, breathing in the perfumed softness of her skin. His lips moved along her collarbone, nibbling gently at her flesh, and she shivered with ecstasy.

'Damn the cocktail party,' her husband whispered huskily. 'I could phone and say we'll be late. I'll tell them the woman tempted me!'

'Why should I take the blame?' she chuckled, twisting around to kiss him. His watch strap caught in her hair and he paused to disentangle it, inadvertently catching sight of its face. 'Good lord, it's six-thirty,' he exclaimed. 'We'll have to go. But we can always continue this later ...' and he gave her one last lingering kiss.

Nevertheless, they were about half an hour late when they entered the vast foyer of the hotel where the reception was to be held (it was one of Stuart's concrete and glass hotels, Andrea was amused to notice), and were directed to the main ballroom. From within came the muffled roar of many voices. Not until then did it occur to Andrea that she was about to be introduced to the cream of New York society; she would cease to be the wife of Stuart Trent, ranch owner, and would appear instead as wife of Simon Ward, famous playwright, a celebrity. It was a daunting prospect, and for a moment she hung back, frightened. But then from her subconscious there was projected an image of that terrifying moment before a skater steps out on the empty sheet of ice to become the focus of a thousand eyes; she drew on her years of training, took two deep breaths, and raised her proud young head.

'Let's take 'em by storm,' Stuart muttered in her ear, and she flashed him a grateful grin, aware that as usual he had understood her feelings. So they were smiling as they entered the ballroom and did indeed become the focus of most eyes.

Milton Wallace came forward with his wife, followed by a succession of directors, actors and actresses, businessmen, and wealthy patrons of the arts, most of whom Andrea never did sort out. The party became a bewildering kaleidoscope of superbly dressed women, their tuxedoed escorts, potent cocktails, delicious canapés, and noise,

noise, noise . . . inside their delicate silver sandals, her feet ached.

But when Stuart said, 'Andrea, I'd like you to meet an old friend of mine,' her smile was as unforced and genuine as it had been an hour (and many introductions) earlier. The woman standing unnecessarily close to her husband, with one beringed hand stroking his sleeve, was without a doubt the most gorgeous creature Andrea had ever seen. A head of flaming red hair, and eyes of a brilliant and unusual jade green; a voluptuous figure clad in a skin-tight white dress that Andrea would not have had the courage to wear; and at her ears, around her throat and wrist, and glimmering in the deep vee of her gown, emeralds as barbaric—and expensive—as the woman herself.

'Cecile, this is my wife, Andrea,' said Stuart. 'Andrea, Cecile Martin—a fellow Albertan.' He smiled teasingly at the flamboyant redhead. 'Although you're such a jet-setter these days, we don't often see you in Alberta.'

Cecile pouted her full red lips provocatively. 'I didn't realise you missed me. If I'd known you were getting married, all the wild horses in Alberta wouldn't have kept me away . . .' and for an instant she darted a look of pure venom at Andrea. 'How long will you be in New York, Stuart honey?'

With that familiar gesture Andrea so loved, Stuart raked his long fingers through his hair. 'Too long, I'm afraid! I hope no more than a month.'

'Then I expect we'll see more of each other,' Cecile said gaily. 'Are you invited to the opening of the Egyptian exhibition at the museum tomorrow night?'

'Yes, gilt-edged invitations,' Stuart concurred. 'Andrea's looking forward to it, aren't you, sweetheart?'

His wife had been standing silently by his side during this exchange, the words 'Martin' and 'fellow Albertan' resounding in her ears. 'Martin' was not an uncommon name in their area; it had to be coincidence. Besides, there was no possible resemblance between the flamboyant Cecile and Ronald's blond sleekness. She suddenly realised Stuart was looking at her rather strangely, waiting for an answer to his question—it was about time he paid her a little attention, she thought resentfully. 'Yes, I am.' Deliberately she tucked her hand into his sleeve, leaning her head against his shoulder. 'As we've only been married three weeks, everywhere I go with Stuart is exciting,' she said demurely.

Cecile's eyes narrowed, cat-like. 'Where did you meet Stuart, Andrea?'

Stuart interposed, covering his wife's hand with his own, 'In the middle of a blizzard, eh, sweetheart?' He grinned at Cecile. 'Sorry, that's rather a private joke. To cut a long story short, Andrea was adrift in a snowstorm between Stony Pass and Valleyfield, and I was lucky enough to find her.'

'Stony Pass?' repeated Cecile reflectively. 'Had you lived in the West for long?'

'No, only six months. I'm from Nova Scotia,' Andrea replied, afraid that with every word she was drawing a noose tighter around her neck. Whether or not Cecile was Ronald's sister, she was a woman who spelled danger to Andrea, of that she was sure.

'Do tell me—what was your name before you were married?' Cecile continued.

'Andrea MacKinlay, of course,' Stuart said breezily, apparently unaware of the undercurrents in the conversation. 'You used to follow figure skating on television, didn't you, Cecile?'

'So that's why you look familiar,' said Cecile, adding insincerely, 'Well, I must congratulate you on your marriage, Andrea. You won't mind if I borrow your husband for a few minutes, will you? I'd like him to meet a friend of mine—an actor, Stuart—he'd be splendid in your new play.' And without waiting for Andrea's reply, she led Stuart away.

Andrea watched them disappear into the crowd, her throat tight with tension. Was Cecile Ronald's sister, or wasn't she? She jumped as Milton touched her arm, intending to introduce her to one of the directors of the museum. Glad of the diversion, she tried to push the problem out of her mind, but in spite of herself her eyes kept sweeping the crowded room, searching for her husband. Then her heart gave a sickening lurch as she saw, making his way purposefully towards her through the press of guests, a slim well-dressed man with sleek blond hair . . . Ronald Martin.

'Excuse me,' she gasped to Milton. 'Can you tell me where the powder room is?'

'Over there, Andrea,' he replied, fortunately pointing in the opposite direction to the approaching Ronald. She wriggled her way through the crowd, conscious of a sense of impending catastrophe, and wanting only to escape, cowardly though that might be, from the heat and the raised voices and the claustrophobic crush of bodies. Not entirely sure where Milton had meant, she went along a short corridor and tried the door on the left. It was unlocked. Shutting it behind her, she leaned against its smooth wood . . . at least she was alone. It was not the powder room, but appeared to be some sort of a private suite, consisting of a small bathroom, a luxurious living area, and an ornately furnished bedroom.

She powdered her nose, trying to rub a little colour into her pale cheeks, then sat down at a small mahogany table, resting her head on her hands. Why, oh, why hadn't she told Stuart about the Martins, and about her ignominious dismissal? She had meant to after they were married, but somehow the golden halcyon days had drifted by and it had slipped to the back of her mind, unimportant beside her newly discovered happiness.

The door of the suite opened. She looked up, her brown eyes huge in her startled face. It was Ronald. As tense as a wild animal finally cornered by a predator, she said, 'Get out!'

He closed the door and walked towards her down the narrow hallway, blocking off, she realised sickly, her only avenue of escape. 'How beautiful to see you again, Andrea,' he said smoothly. 'I was just talking to Cecile and she told me you're married to the great Stuart Trent. Congratulations, my dear. You achieved something Cecile wasn't able to do.'

She got to her feet and backed away from him, mesmerised by the malice in his pale blue eyes; his words slurred enough for her to detect that he had been drinking heavily. In her panic, she did not think of the direction in which she was retreating, her only desire being to widen the distance between them. Her knees collided with something, which to her horror she saw was the bed. She ran around it to the far side. 'Don't come any closer, Ronald,' she warned, keeping her voice steady with an effort. 'I'll scream the place down.'

'Don't you notice how quiet it is in here? Soundproofed, dear Andrea,' he said, taking sadistic pleasure in her fear. He walked around the foot of the bed towards her, and not until he grasped her arm did she break from her terrified trance.

In one lithe movement she twisted away from him, attempting to escape across the width of the bed, but she was hampered by her long gown and fell instead, her body crushed into the mattress by his weight, her hands trapped under his chest. His lips clamped on hers with a bruising force that she was helpless to resist.

To anyone watching there would have been no signs of a struggle: instead there would have been a couple interlocked in an intimate embrace on the bed; and so it must have appeared to Stuart as he burst open the door, and stared through into the bedroom.

Ronald looked up and with undignified haste scrambled to the floor, attempting to straighten his bow tie as he did so. 'Sorry, old man,' he said with an uneasy bravado, 'but really, you know, Andrea does rather keep throwing herself at me. Puts me in an awkward——'

'Get out!' Stuart snarled. 'And if I ever see you near my wife again, I'll break every bone in your body!'

Abandoning Andrea to her fate, Ronald beat a hasty retreat, still fumbling with his disarranged evening clothes. The door shut behind him with a sharp click that penetrated Andrea's frozen calm. 'Stuart, thank God you came!'

'Shut up!' he said brutally.

She gasped. Never had he spoken to her with such bitter

contempt. Scrambling to a sitting position, she stretched out one hand in silent appeal.

Ignoring her mute gesture, he grated, 'Go in the bathroom and do something with your hair and your face. You look like the tramp you are. And then we'll go back to the party and hope no one else will realise what's been going on. Or do you want to be the talk of New York society?'

Her voice box seemed to be totally paralysed. Warily keeping her distance from him, for she did not think it would take much to snap his tenuous self-control, she did as she was told, attempting to repair the damages Ronald had wreaked on her appearance. Then in a strained silence she walked back into the crowded ballroom with her husband to face the most difficult performance of her life—that of presenting a convincing portrait of a happy new bride to people of no mean intelligence and discernment. Somehow she managed ... The party finally came to an end, and feeling utterly drained, she preceded Stuart down the hotel steps, blinking in the glare of flash-bulbs from the gathering of reporters. She was aware that Stuart had, incredibly, made some sort of joke to them, because they laughed and good-naturedly parted their ranks to let her through.

The leather-scented darkness of Stuart's Mercedes enveloped her as a welcome sanctuary. She subsided into her seat, eyeing her husband's uncompromising profile in the glow of light from the dashboard. He was driving with a purely mechanical skill, so preoccupied that she might just as well not have been present. Tentatively she placed her cold fingers on his thigh, for she usually rested them there when they drove together.

With cold precision he put her hand back in her lap, as though it were some distasteful object. 'Don't worry,' he said with heavy sarcasm, 'we'll talk when we get back to the apartment. Perhaps you'd better be thinking up some excuses—I'll be interested to hear them.'

She felt as though she was being drawn deeper and deeper into an inescapable nightmare, a greedy quicksand that would smother her, obliterating her as though she had never been. This misunderstanding, so much her own fault, must not be allowed to tear asunder the whole fabric of their marriage, she vowed, yet was possessed by a blind terror that it would be so.

It was almost a relief when at last they were alone in the quiet apartment, that was so high above the ground that not even the ceaseless roar of traffic reached them. Keeping her evening cloak around her shoulders for warmth, Andrea bent to loosen her sandals.

'Don't bother with that,' Stuart said tartly. 'What I have to say won't take long.'

'Stuart, please——'

'You little bitch,' he said with an almost complete lack of emotion in his voice. 'You really had me fooled, didn't you? How you and Ronald must have laughed at me—the complaisant husband par excellence!'

'You're talking as though I've been having an affair with Ronald,' she broke in, too agitated to remain silent any longer.

'Don't be obtuse. That's exactly what I'm saying.'

'I haven't, Stuart, truly I haven't. You've got to believe me!' she cried passionately.

For the first time since they had entered the apartment, raw anger broke through his veneer of control. 'Then why the hell did you never tell me that you worked for the Martins before you came to me? I'm your husband and I didn't even know that about you.'

Because this was the one question she could not answer, she submerged her guilt in fury. 'I suppose Cecile lost no time in telling you that,' she accused.

'How do you think I felt when I found out that you'd been there for over six months?'

'What else did she have to say?' Andrea demanded, recklessly determined to get the whole sorry mess into the open.

'She related a very convincing story of how you'd been fired for trying to seduce her brother.' He paused, lines of bitter irony scoring his face. 'But I didn't believe her. In fact, I laughed at her, and said she was crazy, you wouldn't do a thing like that. I still trusted you then, you see.'

'I didn't try to seduce him,' she denied frantically, 'but the whole time he was there, he wouldn't leave me alone.'

'I might have believed that earlier this evening. But it's too late now, Andrea. From where Cecile and I were standing in the ballroom, we saw you enter that private suite of rooms, and then we saw Ronald follow—Cecile felt she should explain that you and Ronald had arranged to meet there.'

'We didn't!'

He continued as if she hadn't spoken, 'So I decided to investigate. You certainly didn't waste much time getting down to essentials, did you?'

'He'd been drinking, Stuart,' she protested, knowing it was useless to argue, but desperately trying to convince him of the truth. 'I was trying to get away from him.'

'It didn't look that way to me.' With a muffled groan he buried his head in his hands. In the lamplight his hair gleamed black as coal; she ached to touch its glossy thickness. 'Andrea, why did you have to do this to me?'

'I haven't done anything! But you've chosen to believe Cecile rather than me.'

'I believed the evidence of my own eyes. You and Barbara would have made a good pair—so beautiful on the outside, yet so treacherous on the inside.'

This seemed the cruellest cut of all. Utterly spent, Andrea leaned back in her chair and closed her eyes. 'I can't fight you any more, Stuart,' she said wearily. He got up and left the room, and from their bedroom she heard the opening and shutting of drawers. She ran to the door. 'What . . . what are you doing?'

His eyes like stones, he said, 'I'll sleep in the dressing-room tonight. Oddly enough, I don't think I can stand to share a bed with you. Good night, Andrea.'

CHAPTER SIX

THE door clicked shut behind him. It was several minutes before Andrea realised she was crying, two streams of tears coursing silently down her cheeks; she had never felt such utter desolation before. She pressed her hands to her eyes, willing herself to stop weeping.

Because the embroidered brocade of her dress was now patched and stained with dampness, she slowly took it off and put on her nightclothes, her movements awkward and fumbling. All thought had ceased, leaving only a vast and arid desert of loneliness and fear and pain.

It was a long time before she slept, and when she did it was a sleep haunted by nightmares; at one point she woke to hear her own voice, broken and pleading, calling for Stuart, and late in the night her consciousness was penetrated by the sound of him pacing, restless and driven, up and down his room. But he did not come to her, and it was more than she could do to go to him, for the thought of his total rejection of her was unbearable.

Eventually morning came, a dull grey light filtering through the heavy curtains. For several minutes Andrea lay rigid in her bed, her tired brain reliving the catastrophic events of last night. But with dawn had come new hope. It now seemed impossible that the rift between her and Stuart would last; somehow she would be able to repair it, convince him that she was innocent of any involvement with Ronald.

She splashed cold water on her face and brushed her hair loose on her shoulders, then belted her robe tightly around her waist. However, on her way to the kitchen she paused a moment in consternation—Stuart was talking to someone. Quietly she pushed open the swing door.

He was on the telephone, his voice heavy and lifeless, his back turned towards her. 'Flight 747,' he was saying,

writing the numbers on a scrap of paper on the table.
'Leaves here at one-forty-five this afternoon ... yes, I'll
pick the ticket up at the airport an hour ahead of time.
Thanks very much. Goodbye.'

He hung up, and as he did so, saw her standing as still as
a statue by the door. But he said nothing, pouring himself a
cup of coffee and sitting down at the table with it, his lean
fingers curving around the mug as he stared at some
imaginary pattern traced in the tension-filled air. And although questions were clamouring in her throat, Andrea
found herself unable to speak either, terrified that her
voice would reveal the fragility of her composure.

It seemed an age before Stuart lifted eyes that were as
cold and hard as stone. 'I've made reservations for you to
go back to Calgary this afternoon. You can go on to White
Birches from there.' His tone brooked neither comment nor
argument; he had delivered an order.

'But you ... you haven't finished your work here, Stuart,
how can you leave now?' Andrea questioned shakily.

'I have no intention of leaving yet. If you had listened
more carefully, you would have heard that I said *you* will
be returning. I shall stay here until I complete what I came
to do.' His voice was sharp, his eyes revealing a mixture of
anger and bitter distaste.

'Oh, Stuart, please ... let's talk this out. You don't
understand, you——' she was not allowed to finish. He
slammed a fist on the table, looking as though he would
prefer to direct his violence at her.

'No, Andrea! It's you who don't understand.' Shoving
back his chair, he seized her by the arms, his fingers biting
into her soft flesh.

'Stop it, Stuart ... you're hurting me .. stop it!' Her
voice broke in a half sob, and she struggled to hold back
the tears.

He gave a mocking laugh. 'I'm hurting you! Poor Andrea
... my poor misunderstood Andrea.' She cried out with
pain as his fingers increased their cruel hold.

'Now listen to what I have to say, and listen carefully,'
he grated. 'You're going back to White Birches and there

you'll stay until I return. And God help you and your precious Ronald if he so much as sets foot on my property!'

His voice blazed white-hot in her ears, as her mind whirled with the terrifying implications of what he was saying.

'Stuart, please listen. Please . . .' she pleaded weakly.

He continued as if she had never spoken. 'I did a lot of thinking last night, Andrea, my dear.' She covered her ears with shaking hands to blot out the sarcasm of his endearment, but he shook her mercilessly and shouted, 'Listen to me! It would no doubt be logical if I took steps to obtain a divorce. But there will be no divorce, Andrea. Do you hear me?—no divorce! You'll go back to White Birches and there you will be a mother to my children and a wife to me. I won't have a repeat performance of what I went through with Barbara, so you are not to see Ronald Martin again—ever!'

She shrank away from him, appalled by the depths of his hatred.

A sneer twisted his mouth. 'You don't like that ultimatum? Well, that's too bad, because I mean every word I say. You're my wife and you'll remain my wife, but you won't disgrace me or my name, or by God you'll suffer the consequences!'

He flung her from him with a force that revealed the violence of his emotions, and strode from the kitchen.

Andrea feebly stumbled to a chair and sat down. She rubbed her bruised arms, while again bitter tears streamed down her pale face as she wept for the pain that seemed to grip her very soul. Overnight Stuart's love had changed to a raging, all-consuming enmity, and she now belonged to a man who would hold her to him, not with love, but with hate. She buried her head in her arms, wondering desperately how she could ever make him see the truth, or understand what had really happened. It seemed an impossible task.

That afternoon at the airport Stuart parked the Mercedes on the ramp and in silence he and Andrea threaded their way through the ranks of cars towards the terminal.

In cruel mockery of her feelings, it was a beautiful day, clear and sunny, a flirtatious breeze preventing the warmth from becoming oppressive. A jet screamed overhead, leaving twin trails of exhaust white against the azure sky.

Automatically courteous, Stuart held the glass door open for her, and she preceded him into the building, its air-conditioned chill making her shiver. After he had picked up the ticket and checked her baggage, they still had forty minutes to wait. Forty minutes ... Andrea longed for the time to be over, yet dreaded her departure with equal intensity.

'Come on. We'll get a coffee,' Stuart said brusquely, apparently finding the forced inactivity as difficult to cope with as she.

'Why are you waiting?' she asked in sudden vexation. 'You don't have to worry, I'll get on the plane.'

'I thought I made it abundantly clear yesterday that I no longer believe a word you say.'

There seemed to be nothing she could add to this. She choked down half a cup of black coffee and then pushed it away, her eyes wandering abstractedly around the crowded restaurant. Less than a month ago, at the airport in Calgary, she and Stuart had waved goodbye to Cynthia, and he had kissed her with love and passion and had carried her away to his mountain retreat. And now, from halfway across the continent, he was sending her home in disgrace, his love for her ruined, all their bright hopes destroyed. She swallowed hard, too proud to cry in front of him, instead fiercely concentrating her attention on a mother whose small son had just upset his milk all over the table.

'Are you finished?' Stuart had to repeat his question twice before she heard him. She looked at him, still only half comprehending, her eyes blind with pain. He gave an incoherent exclamation, and for a fleeting instant her own pain was reflected in his eyes. His hand, of its own volition, reached out towards her across the table. But then, equally suddenly, he withdrew it, his eyes again granite-hard. He pushed back his chair with a suppressed violence that tore at the edges of her self-control. 'Let's get out of here,' he growled.

The bored voice of the announcer came over the loudspeaker above them. 'Flight 747, jet service to Montreal, Toronto, Winnipeg and Calgary now boarding at Gate 51. All aboard. No smoking, please.'

The words sounded like a death knell. This couldn't be happening, Andrea thought frantically, it couldn't. 'Stuart,' she said urgently, 'please don't send me away. I can't bear to go——'

'Be quiet!' he ordered savagely. 'We're finished, Andrea. Get that through your head, once and for all. Love can survive a great deal, but not the kind of thing you've done with Ronald.'

He had taken her arm, his fingers digging through her sleeve, and was steering her urgently through the throngs of people towards their destination. Passengers were already trickling through Gate 51 and out on to the runway, where an immense silver jet was waiting in the sun ... waiting to carry her away from Stuart. And at the last moment, from reserves of strength she did not know she possessed, she was able to confront her husband's flint-like face and say with quiet dignity, 'Goodbye, Stuart. Take care of yourself.'

He stared at her, his grey eyes inscrutable. Then, with shocking suddenness, he kissed her hard on the mouth, wheeled, and walked away from her, never once looking back.

This gesture, so totally unexpected, was Andrea's undoing. Tears flooded her eyes. She blinked them back, fumbling for a handkerchief ... there would be plenty of time for tears at the ranch.

But that evening when she finally reached White Birches, and was feeling more alone than she had ever felt in her life before, still the tears would not flow. The most difficult thing she had ever done was to enter the bedroom she and Stuart had shared so briefly; naturally enough, that was where Maggie had carried her suitcases. It was late at night, and she was so physically and mentally exhausted that she had passed the point where she could sleep, or even relax; a solid lump of misery in her throat, she paced up and down the room, memories cruelly battering at her fragile defences. Stuart's kisses, his urgent caresses, his hard body arousing her to an intensity of passion that had made them one in body and soul ... the recollection of this perfect oneness made her present loneliness all the more impossible to bear.

It was nearly dawn before she finally flung herself across the bed and buried her face in the pillow, hard choking sobs wrenched from her throat. The cool linen soaked up the tears and muffled her sobs. Gradually they diminished in intensity, until the blessed oblivion of sleep claimed her.

In the days that followed, Maggie and Clayton, if they were surprised to see her home without her husband, were too tactful to show it. Even so, Andrea found herself avoiding them, unable to face their unspoken questions or poorly disguised concern. The ranch, basking in the early June sun, was incredibly beautiful, and she spent hours on long solitary walks along the trails that wound through the woods, catching glimpses of the distant mountains through the curtains of rustling poplar leaves. Down by the creek, perched on the rocks, she watched patiently until the majestic moose came to drink in the rippling stream; high over the meadows, she saw the hawks hang poised, searching for prey. The air was alive with bird-song. Gophers and magpies, elk and rabbits ... she saw them all, and somehow gained comfort from their unobtrusive presence.

The first terrible night alone in Stuart's bed had drained the worst of her grief; she was left with a continual dull ache, so that she moved through the hours and days in a kind of daze, only partly alive. But after she had been home for nearly two weeks, two things happened that eroded this brittle peace.

It was the end of term; she drove to Calgary in the Mercedes to bring Heather and Bruce home for the summer. The sight of the school, high brick walls mellow in the

sun, brought its quota of bittersweet memories . . . the day
of the skating party, when she had met the children for the
first time; the weekends she and Stuart had come here to
get the twins, and she had basked in the delight of her new-
found family. And now, walking into the hallway alone, she
braced herself for the inevitable questions.

'Hi, Andrea!' Heather cried, spotting her first. 'Where's
Daddy?'

Bruce came running too, and planted an untidy kiss on
Andrea's cheek. 'No more school until September!' he
crowed. 'Is Dad in the car?'

'Your father is still in New York,' Andrea explained,
adding hastily as she saw their little faces fall, 'He'll be
back in a week or so, I'm sure. He had to stay, and I know
he's missing you both.'

They seemed to accept her explanation. To divert them,
Andrea said, 'Tomorrow I'll take you down to the creek
after supper, and we'll see the moose—there's a baby one
who comes with the mother every night. And once the
ponies come, Clayton's going to take you on an all day
ride, and cook your lunch on a campfire.'

Her tactics were successful, and in the next few days
only occasionally did one or the other of the children say, 'I
wish Dad was here,' or, 'Did you hear when Dad's coming
back?' Since Andrea had not had as much as a letter or a
phone call from Stuart since she had left New York, this
last question was especially difficult to answer, but she
managed somehow. She had come to love Stuart's children
for themselves, but now that she was estranged from their
father, there were times when their heart-stopping resemblance to Stuart was almost more than she could bear.
Still, on the whole, their company was good for her, and
accompanying them on their usually strenuous pursuits at
least tired her out sufficiently that she was able to sleep.

But the second event destroyed her tenuous hold on
normality. A letter arrived from Cynthia. As Andr   )ened
it a bundle of press cuttings fell to the floor. She picked
them up and unfolded them. They were clippings from the
society pages of the *New York Times*, one comp..te with a

photograph of a group of people in evening dress, two of whom were Stuart and Cecile.

A wave of dizziness swept over Andrea; she groped for a chair and sat down, her eyes riveted on Stuart's image. He looked handsome and at ease, and at the moment when the photographer had snapped the picture had been laughing at something Cecile must have said. Cecile herself was glamorously dressed in a low-cut gown decorated with sequins. Barely noticing the others in the photo, Andrea moved to the printed clippings, which Cynthia had heavily underlined in red pencil ... 'Mr Stuart Trent and Miss Cecile Martin attended the opening night of *La Traviata* ... the playwright, Simon Ward, was present at a luncheon given by the New York Authors' Club, and was accompanied by his constant companion, Miss Cecile Martin ...'

Fighting for control, Andrea bunched the papers into a ball and flung them into the fireplace. But this violent action could not erase the torturing mental image of Cecile's air of smug possessiveness, or of Stuart's casual laughter. A piercing jealousy attacked her, digging its sharp claws deep into her being. It was several minutes before she recovered sufficiently to read Cynthia's letter. Its gist was largely what she would have expected; her aunt, puzzled and upset by the articles she had enclosed, wanted an immediate explanation of what was going on, and advised that Andrea fight Cecile on her own ground, rather than by running back to the ranch like a scared rabbit.

But then, thought Andrea grimly, Cynthia didn't know that Andrea had not run away, but had instead been ordered home by her husband; fortunately that little titbit appeared to have escaped the reporters.

'Lunch time, Andrea!' Heather called.

'Coming!' She shoved the letter into her handbag and got to her feet. Her vision blurred momentarily and the room swayed. By lowering her head and shutting her eyes, the brief dizziness disappeared, and cautiously she moved away from the chair; she couldn't get sick now, she thought with dismay, for it took all her strength to cope with the children and the daily routine as it was. So she made a valiant effort to eat Maggie's delicious lunch, and afterwards went for her usual afternoon riding lesson with Clayton.

She was not aware of looking any different from what she had the past few days, but after one quick glance at her, Clayton said abruptly, 'Andrea, I know damn well it's none of my business, and you can tell me to get lost if you want to—but you look like you've been dragged through a knothole backwards. What's wrong?'

She smiled at him mistily, touched by his rough and ready sympathy, and longing to confide in him. 'Oh dear,' she said unsteadily, 'is it that obvious?'

'Yeah.'

They had mounted and were jogging side by side along the corral fence towards the pastureland. Andrea stared down at the saddlehorn, and said finally, 'I guess I miss Stuart.' This, of course, was true, as far as it went.

'Why isn't he home here where he belongs?'

'He had to work on the play,' she replied defensively.

'Sure,' Clayton scoffed. 'Come clean. What really happened in New York, Andrea?'

She temporised, 'We had a fight—but I expect every marriage must have its rough patches.'

'Three weeks after the wedding?'

They had slowed to a walk, the horses ambling along the bank of the creek, the squeak of leather and jingle of bit accompanying their low-voiced conversation. 'Stuart thinks I—committed adultery with Ronald Martin,' Andrea said baldly. 'He found us together in circumstances that must have looked pretty convincing—but there's not a word of truth in it, Clayton. I love Stuart.' She spoke with a passionate intensity. 'I'd die rather than be unfaithful to him.'

'Okay, okay,' her companion said gently. 'You don't have to convince me—I believe you. I've heard about young Martin; he has quite a reputation as a ladykiller around these parts. How did you manage to get tangled up with the likes of him?'

'I'd better tell you the whole story.' And so she related to him the events of the last three months, how she had been dismissed from the Martins, and had hidden the truth from Stuart, how she and Ronald had met again so briefly and so disastrously at the party in New York. She ended with how Stuart had compelled her to return to the ranch alone.

Clayton was silent for a few moments after she had finished, his far-sighted blue eyes gazing unseeingly at the green stretch of prairie ahead of them, his hands loose on the reins. 'When's Stuart coming home?' he asked finally.

'I don't know. I haven't heard from him.'

'When he does get back, I'll have a word with him about this mess. He usually pays attention to what I have to say.' There was a grim note in Clayton's normally peaceable voice.

'Oh, no, you can't do that,' Andrea protested, horrified. 'He'd never forgive me for confiding in anyone else.'

'It seems to me he might not forgive you anyway. Besides, I'm not just "anyone else". I've known Stuart since he was knee-high to a grasshopper. Someone'll have to do something, Andrea. He can be mighty mule-headed, that husband of yours.'

'If only he'd listened to me,' she said miserably. 'I tried to explain, but I don't think he heard a word I said.'

'That, my dear, is a legacy from Barbara,' Clayton replied grimly. 'If you'd have tried, you couldn't have done anything that would have infuriated Stuart more than to be found in a bedroom with Ronald. Barbara used to bring her men-friends to the ranch, you know, whenever she thought Stuart's back was turned. But of course he knew perfectly well what was going on. Because of the twins, he stifled his pride and tried to pretend nothing was wrong. God knows what that must have cost him.'

She closed her eyes, rubbing her forehead with tense fingers. 'And now he thinks I'm cast in the same mould.'

'He's a fool if he believes that. You and Barbara are as different as day and night. You must let me speak to him, Andrea, you can't go on like this. You don't even look well.'

'I have been feeling dreadfully tired,' she admitted. 'But please don't say anything to Stuart, Clayton. We'll work it out somehow. Promise you won't?'

Reluctantly he nodded. 'If you say so. But I can't say I agree with your decision.'

Inexpressibly comforted by having shared the burden of the past few weeks, Andrea smiled at the older man. 'I'll race you to the creek,' she suggested, a glint of the old mischief in her eye.

Half an hour later, after a lively ride, they arrived back at the ranch. Clayton disappeared to do his chores while Andrea dismounted. To her consternation, as her feet hit the ground, her knees buckled and the wooden walls of the stall dipped and swayed. Feeling icy cold, she clung to the saddle, her face buried in Star's warm flank. Slowly the faintness passed. She straightened, drawing a deep, shuddering breath.

What on earth was wrong with her? she wondered, suddenly overwhelmed by a desperate longing for the security and comfort of Stuart's presence, for the warmth of his arm hard around her waist . . . her loneliness was intensified by the memory of the intimacy they had shared so short a time ago. Was Stuart even now giving Cecile the same heartwarming tenderness he had given her? She closed her mind to the harrowing images this evoked, and busied herself rubbing down Star with a handful of straw, and putting away the tack.

The following day a double horse trailer arrived from Calgary with the children's ponies aboard. They were both pintoes, their coats splashed with patches of black and white and brown. Under Clayton's watchful eyes, the twins had their first ride in the corral, while Andrea perched on the fence watching them. The ponies were tractable little creatures, well-trained and sweet-tempered, and the twins were delighted with them, heeding every word of Clayton's soft-spoken instructions. Within a week they were able to accompany Andrea and Clayton on short rides across the prairie.

It had been a quiet week for Andrea. She no longer watched the mail for letters from her husband, nor did she jump every time the phone rang, hoping she would hear his beloved voice. She was still occasionally troubled by spasms of dizziness, and found she was sleeping a great deal in an effort to combat the leaden tiredness that weighed down her limbs and turned small everyday jobs into gargantuan tasks. Despite the hours she spent in the sun, her face refused to tan, while smudges of weariness shadowed her eyes. She knew she should go to a doctor, but procrastinated; her accident had left her with a deep-rooted reluctance to visit the medical profession, which she recognised as unfair but found impossible to overcome. So she kept to her regular routine as much as possible, expending most of her energy with the children.

Then, three weeks after Andrea had returned to the ranch, everything changed. She and the children were coming back from their ride. They emerged from the leaf-shadowed tunnel of the trail into the dazzling sunlight; temporarily blinded, Andrea did not at first see the tall figure waiting in the shade by the stables.

'Daddy!' Heather screamed, forgetting all Clayton's carefully instilled lessons as she scrambled off the pony's back, landing with a thud in the dust. She picked herself up and ran towards her father, Bruce close behind her. Slowly Andrea dismounted, her fingers stiff and awkward as she looped the halter over her arm and gathered up the ponies' neglected reins.

The moment that she had so often anticipated had finally arrived—her husband had come home. As she walked to the stable, the scene burned itself into her brain for ever ... the white-painted building, surrounded by neatly clipped green grass; the two children running pell-mell towards their father, who was visibly bracing himself for their tumultuous welcome; three black heads gleaming in the sun; the old feeling of being left out, of being alone ...

Since there was nothing else she could do, she approached them, her footsteps silent on the turf. She felt detached from her body: from somewhere in space she watched a young woman lead two ponies into the shade of a stable.

Stuart straightened. He was wearing tan-coloured whip-cord trousers with a cream silk shirt, an ascot tucked into the neck. He looked cool and composed; Andrea was abruptly made aware of her wind-tousled hair and dusty jeans.

The smile with which he had greeted his children faded; his eyes were as granite-hard as the mountains, and his expression made her recoil as surely as a physical blow would have done. But, just when it seemed inevitable that the twins would sense the tension between the two adults, his lips re-shaped a smile that did not reach his eyes, and he said lightly, 'Hello, Andrea. We'll save our greetings until later, shall we?'

'You're supposed to kiss her, Daddy,' Heather protested in a disappointed tone.

'I guess you're right,' he drawled, pulling Andrea into his arms. He smelled of soap and after-shave, and the warmth of his skin seeped through her thin shirt. For a moment, conquered by forces beyond her control, she melted in his embrace. Instinctively his arms tightened their hold, and his heartbeat quickened. Her hands, of their own volition, slid up his chest and around his neck, and she raised her face to his, her eyes already closed. Their lips met and clung with all the sweetness and ardour she so well remembered.

Then, with all his strength, Stuart pushed her away. Scarcely able to stand, Andrea saw his eyes glittering with self-disgust and with an emotion she recognised incredulously as hate. So softly that only the two of them could hear, he said, 'Up to your old tricks again, dear wife? Well, this time they won't work. And now, shall we behave like two loving parents for the next few hours?' Although he had couched it as a question, it was plainly an order.

Fortunately for Andrea, he turned from her to the ponies, and in the ensuing flurry of excitement as the twins demonstrated their new skills, she was able to recover, at least outwardly, some of her composure. She unsaddled and groomed Star, finding solace in the simple and mechanical task. The mare nuzzled her with velvet-smooth nostrils, as the girl gave her one last affectionate rub between the ears. Then Andrea quietly headed for the stable door, hoping to leave without being noticed by the trio at the other end of the building.

'Where are you going, Andrea?' Stuart asked.

'She always has a nap after our ride,' Heather piped. ' 'Cos she gets tired.'

'Oh? What do you mean—tired?'

'I just seem to need a lot of sleep lately, that's all,' said Andrea defensively. 'I'll see you all at supper.' And she made her escape quickly before Stuart could say anything further.

Stuart's suitcases were heaped in one corner of their bedroom. Andrea stared at them as she might have stared at an interloper. Maggie, of course, was responsible for that. Or had Stuart requested they be put here? Was he going to sleep in this room, and share her bed again?

When she had met him outside the stable, there had been that heart-stopping instant when their lips had met and their bodies had fused ... but then Stuart had thrust her away, and the bitter anger in his eyes had cut her to the quick ... she stripped off her riding clothes, leaving them in a heap on the floor, and showered, then slid between the cool sheets, knowing she would never sleep but at least could rest.

An hour later she wakened, not to a sound but to a presence. Struggling out of the depths of a slumber so deep as to seem almost drugged, she focused with difficulty on the man standing at the end of the bed. 'What's the time?' she asked listlessly. 'I must have slept after all. Am I late for supper?'

He said nothing, but simply stood there, gazing at her. Abruptly she realised that beneath the silky sheets she was naked. A blush crept up her throat to her cheeks until she felt scorched with its heat. To break the silence she said, 'Is dinner ready?'

'In half an hour. The children are having their baths before they get changed. We'll all eat together. It goes without saying that I expect you to play your part well.

Andrea. After all, deception comes easily to you, doesn't it?'

In one swift movement Andrea sat up in bed, remembering just in time to hold on to the sheet. The evening sun, slanting through the west window, touched her bare shoulders with gold. Quite suddenly she was fully awake—fully awake and gloriously angry. 'Remarks like that certainly won't help me play the part!'

He walked around the foot of the bed towards her. His broad-shouldered bulk came between her and the sun, and she looked up at him in sudden alarm, clutching the fragile protection of the sheet more closely to her breast. 'I'll make any remarks I like,' he said with a deliberate slowness that held a subtle threat.

Wanting only to hurt him, she said cruelly, 'Perhaps you'd better consider the effects on your children if you do that.'

His mouth tightened, his gaze bleak as a winter sky. 'You really are contemptible, Andrea, aren't you?' he said conversationally. His eyes raked her body, so inadequately concealed by the sheet. 'Get up and dress. And remember, you'll suffer the consequences if you do anything to hurt those children.'

'Oh, of course, I'm the one to suffer,' she flared. 'Nothing's ever your fault—you're perfect!'

'Don't push me too far,' he warned.

'Why not, Stuart? Are you afraid you might find out you've made a mistake?'

'The only mistake I made was to think you were any different from Barbara.'

'Barbara!' she spat furiously. 'I'm sick of the sound of her name. And I'm sick of being compared to her.'

'Then you shouldn't have behaved like her, should you?'

'I didn't!' Suddenly she shivered, from more than the cold. 'Oh, what's the use, Stuart? Why don't you just let me go?'

'Because of my children,' he answered implacably. 'They still love you, you see.'

'And you don't . . .'

'No.'

The bleak monosyllable convinced her of his sincerity where a tirade of words might not have. Wearily she said, 'I'd better get ready for dinner.'

'Yes, you'd better. And remember what I said, Andrea—play your part well.' On these words he was gone.

Andrea rested her head on her knees, while the reckless flood of anger drained away. He hated her . . . wanting only to lie down and cry her eyes out, she tried to gather the energy to get out of bed and go downstairs for dinner, but the mere thought of food made her feel physically ill, just as the thought of being happy and lighthearted in front of Heather and Bruce filled her with dread and an unutterable weakness of spirit.

It was the clear chiming of the dinner bell that jerked her out of bed. She dragged on the first dress that came to hand, ran a comb through her hair, and hurriedly outlined her mouth with pink lipstick, hoping to minimise her pallor. Shoes, her gold bracelet, and she was ready. She ran down the stairs to the dining-room, and because she had been hurrying there was a little colour in her cheeks and she was able to greet the twins quite naturally.

She even managed to eat a small amount, not noticing that Stuart was watching how much of her food went back to the kitchen. By talking about the ponies, and a planned all-day picnic with Clayton, and the latest kitten family in the stables, she got through the interminable meal somehow. Afterwards, they played rummy and four-handed solitaire around the table. Finally Stuart pushed his chair back. 'Bedtime, you two,' he said firmly to the twins, ignoring their groans of protest. 'Clean your teeth and put on your pyjamas, and I'll read you a story. Andrea's done enough for one day.'

Andrea's lashes flew upwards in surprise, but his expression was totally unreadable. 'I have to do a bit of work in the study,' he said to her. 'Don't wait up for me.'

And what was that supposed to mean? she thought uncertainly. Too restless to sit still, she helped Maggie clear the table and wash up, but it was still only nine o'clock.

Stuart had already shut himself in the study, so she went upstairs to the twins' rooms. They were both asleep—how angelic they looked with their rosy cheeks and tangled curls, and how Bruce would resent being called angelic!

Andrea looked out of the hall window. A full moon hung low in the sky, bathing the hills in a luminous silver light; there was not a breath of wind. Getting her jacket, she slipped out by the side door, and for nearly an hour wandered along the trails near the house. The shadowed woods were quiet and still; to her overwrought imagination there was a waiting quality to the stillness, an ominous sense of expectation. She leaned against the rough trunk of a giant spruce, part of her mind noticing how its fragrant boughs blacked out the stars. Clenching her hands in her pockets, she tried vainly to warm her fingers; her heart was thudding in her breast and there was a tightness in her throat ... 'Don't wait up for me,' Stuart had said ... so was she to sleep alone tonight after all? Or would she be given the chance to repair some of the damage that had been wreaked on their marriage, to recapture some of the intimacy that had been so cruelly sundered? In New York, the morning of her forced departure, Stuart had said, 'You'll be my wife ...' What had he meant?

The questions were unanswerable here in the silent forest; the only way to settle them was to go home, home to her husband.

He was still in the study, because a thin line of light shone under the door. Not knowing whether to be relieved or disappointed, Andrea climbed the stairs to their room, where she slowly undressed and got into bed. Her book failed to hold more than a small portion of her attention, and eventually she laid it face down on the blanket; propped up with pillows, she was gazing into the night's blackness when Stuart opened the door and as quietly closed it behind him.

Still in utter silence, he stared at his wife. Her dark hair, spread across the pillow, shone in the glow of the bedside lamp; her eyes were as wide and frightened as those of a startled deer; unconsciously her slim fingers were kneading the hem of the sheet into a crumpled ball.

'I wasn't expecting to see you here,' she offered finally, her voice thin in the quiet room,

'Why not?' He unknotted his tie and hung it in the cupboard, then started to unbutton his shirt.

Hypnotised, she followed the movements of his hands as he draped the shirt across the back of a chair, and dropped his gold cuff links into an ashtray on the chest of drawers. All his actions were slow and deliberate, their very lack of haste holding a subtle threat. The air between them vibrated with tension, until she thought she would scream.

'I asked you a question, Andrea,' he said. 'Why not?'

Her tongue felt thick in her mouth. 'You've made it quite plain since you got back that you feel nothing but contempt for me—that you despise me. And yet you've come to my bedroom ...'

She shivered under the lash of his steel grey eyes. 'No matter what you've done, you're still my wife. As your husband I have a perfect right to be in your bedroom, I would have thought?'

His cynicism flicked her on the raw. 'Stuart, please believe me,' she begged. 'I did nothing with Ronald— nothing.' Her voice trembled. 'I love you, don't you understand? I'd never be unfaithful to you. It's the last thing I'd do.'

'Andrea,' he answered wearily, 'we've been through all this before. Don't start again, for God's sake.'

He had finished undressing. He turned off the light, in the darkness she felt him climb into the bed beside her. She closed her eyes, more frightened than she had ever been before in her life.

It was well after midnight, and still Andrea was wide awake, her eyes burning with tiredness and with the tears she had shed. Beside her, Stuart's big body slumbered, his breathing harsh. A shudder rippled through her body. They had made love ... although there had been no love in it, she recalled bitterly. 'Hate' would be a better word. There had been no tenderness, no whispered endearments, no

care for her pleasure—he had used her, for his own
physical release. Again she shuddered, engulfed in shame
and despair. How different men and women were, she
thought; to share a bed with someone you hated seemed
inconceivable to her, yet not only had Stuart done it, but
he was apparently unmoved by any of the conflict that was
tearing her to pieces.

After a while she slid out of bed, wrapping her robe
around her, and went to sit by the window. As her eyes
adjusted to the dark, the familiar silhouettes of the trees
and the stables materialised in the gloom—nothing was
changed out there, it was only she who had changed . . .
the golden flame of her happiness transformed into the
grey ashes of bitterness and sorrow.

Several days had passed when Stuart came into the sunroom where Andrea was toying with her breakfast. 'You
don't eat enough,' he began caustically. 'You've lost weight,
which you can scarcely afford to do.'

'Speaking to me like that will hardly increase my appetite,' she snapped. In truth, she was feeling miserable, and
knew her looks reflected her ill-health. Her eyes had mauve
shadows above cheekbones that were unduly prominent in
her thin face. The mere sight of food was enough to upset
her stomach, while she was bothered too by a recurring
dizziness. But the last person in whom she would confide
these symptoms would be her husband; he would undoubtedly accuse her of trying to trade on his sympathy.

He threw a folded white card on the table by her plate.
'Write or phone and let her know we'll be there,' he said
coldly.

She picked it up, and read the few words inscribed on it
in an unmistakably feminine hand; the ink, she noticed
distastefully, was violet, and surely the card was scented?
But it was the message itself that made her palms suddenly
damp . . . Cecile Martin was giving an outdoor barbecue
next Saturday, and would be delighted to have the company of Andrea and Stuart Trent . . .

'I won't go.'

'Oh, yes, you will, my dear.'

She flung the card back on the table. 'It might say the company of Andrea and Stuart Trent, but what it really means is the company of Stuart Trent. I'm not that much of a fool, Stuart.'

'You're being very childish, Andrea.' There was an edge of anger in his voice.

Disregarding it, she swept on. 'It didn't take her long to follow you back to Alberta, did it? How very flattered you must be!'

He slammed his fist on the table so hard that the china rattled and a glass fell on its side. Petrified, Andrea gripped the sides of her chair, even as her brown eyes blazed in mute defiance.

'I don't know what you're trying to say,' he stormed, 'but I know exactly what I'm saying. You're going to the barbecue, Andrea. If I have to drag you there by force, you'll go!'

He looked perfectly capable of carrying out his threat. She tilted her chin proudly. 'You leave me no choice, do you?'

'I'm glad to hear it.' His heavy sarcasm made her flinch. 'Don't forget to answer the invitation.'

He left the room, and gradually her fingers loosened their hold on the chair. She rubbed them absently; they were sore where the wood had scored her flesh. It was useless to defy Stuart, but because her own temper was unpredictable these days, it persisted in flaring up to meet his. She got up to fetch her notepaper—not for anything would she telephone Cecile Martin.

'Finished with your breakfast, dear?' Maggie asked, her faded blue eyes noting how little Andrea had actually eaten.

'Mmm, thanks, Maggie,' Andrea replied, adding apologetically, 'Your cooking is lovely. I guess I just wasn't hungry, though.'

'I'll tempt your appetite later on with my corn chowder and fresh rolls,' the housekeeper said comfortably. 'By the way, Mr Stuart asked me to look after the twins next Saturday. I'm glad you're both going to a party; you've been cooped up at the ranch long enough.'

'It's at the Martins'—a barbecue,' Andrea volunteered.

Maggie tipped her head to one side. 'Funny that Miss Cecile's home now. She usually spends her summer in Scandinavia and France with her friends.'

It's not funny at all, Andrea thought. She's having an affair with my husband, that's why she's home.

But outwardly her composure did not falter. 'Well, I'd better answer the invitation,' she said, and ended the conversation.

The day of the barbecue Andrea had wished for rain, but in mockery of her hopes the sun shone brightly all day. In a mood of grim determination to get through the ordeal with as much dignity as possible, she dressed in slim beige slacks with a matching vest and striped blouse, and left her hair loose on her shoulders, an arrangement which she hoped had the right combination of informality and smartness. A light jacket, against the evening chill, and she was ready.

Stuart was already waiting for her in the car. It gave Andrea a peculiar sensation to be driving to the Martins', back along the road where Stuart had nearly run her over, the road where she had struggled in the snow a few months ago. How drastically her life had changed since then; she had scaled the heights of happiness and fathomed the depths of despair. She stole a glance at her husband's ruthless profile, wondering if he, too, was being assailed by memories of their tempestuous meeting. If so, he gave no hint of it; indeed, he had scarcely spoken a word since they had left.

The sun had set behind the mountains, the peaks black against a roseate sky, by the time the Martins' stone mansion came into view. Coloured lanterns garlanded the trees, adding a fairytale touch to the spacious gardens; in one corner the coals in the barbecue pit glowed dull orange in the dusk. Stuart parked the car and they walked towards the house, Andrea mentally bracing herself for the meeting with Cecile.

Cecile herself ushered them in. 'Hello, Andrea. How nice

to see you again,' she said, without any great pretence at sincerity. Her voice came alive. 'Stuart, honey, how tired you look! I'm afraid New York must agree with you better than Alberta. There are drinks in the den, darling, you know the way. Help yourself and join the others on the patio. I'll take Andrea upstairs so she can leave her jacket there.'

Even though Stuart had seemed barely aware of her presence, still Andrea wished he had not left her alone with Cecile. She trailed up the stairs, again conscious of a leaden tiredness pulling at her limbs; in the bedroom she cursorily ran a comb through her thick hair, one part of her mind registering how pale and washed-out she looked beside Cecile's flamboyant beauty. The redhead was wearing hiphuggers of soft cream buckskin, and a tight-fitting fringed waistcoat; exquisitely tooled leather boots accentuated her height, giving her an unfair advantage over Andrea.

After one swift glance to make sure they were alone in the room, Cecile said with a pitiless calm, 'I've wanted five minutes alone with you ever since we met. That's why I invited you here tonight.'

'I didn't think it was for the pleasure of my company,' Andrea responded drily.

Cecile continued as though Andrea had never spoken. 'I'm going to get Stuart back, Andrea.'

'What do you mean—get him back?'

'I mean just what I say. Stuart is mine. He and I would have been married by now if you hadn't come along and ruined everything. I don't know why he married you— although after what I've heard from Ronald, I can guess. But I do know this—Stuart regrets his marriage, it's not difficult to see that.'

Speechless, Andrea gazed into the other woman's green eyes, that were as hard and brilliant as emeralds. The words echoed and re-echoed in her mind ... regrets his marriage ... regrets his marriage ...

Exasperated, Cecile snapped, 'I don't think you've heard a word I said. I'll say it again—I'm going to get him back,

Andrea. And if you get hurt in the process, that's too bad. There's such a thing as divorce, you know, and next time he'll marry me, not some little nobody from nowhere whom he picked up in a snowstorm.'

Finally Andrea spoke, her small face white and set, her quiet voice invested with a dignity Cecile's had lacked. 'Stuart married me because he loved me,' she said. 'You and your brother have done your best to wreck that love, but you're mistaken if you think Stuart will divorce me. He won't. I'm his wife now, and his wife I'll remain. And there's nothing you can do about it.'

'We'll see about that,' Cecile replied grimly, her perfect features marred by a spasm of pure fury; it was obvious that she had not expected any opposition from Andrea. 'I've never yet met the man I couldn't have—and have on my own terms. So don't think for a minute I'll let a whey-faced little schemer like you stand in my way!'

Andrea brushed a strand of hair away from her face, wondering how much more of this she could stand, and if she was going to faint again; in front of Cecile, that would be the final humiliation. It was with deep relief that she heard Cecile say, 'You can join us on the patio—after you've thought over what I've said,' and saw the redhead storm out of the room. As she sat down on one of the beds, absently twisting the plain gold band on the third finger of her left hand, one thought emerged from the chaos in her mind—was it true, what Cecile had implied? Had she and Staurt been engaged to be married? And if so, why had Stuart never mentioned it to her?

For a moment she covered her face with her hands, overwhelmed by the possibility that Stuart had deceived her and had indeed married her on a whim, a whim he had soon regretted. It couldn't be true, she mused; no man could fake the kind of love Stuart had given her before and after their wedding. In a world now cold and hostile, she had to hold on to that one truth—Stuart had married her for love.

A few minutes later she made her way downstairs and through the lounge to the patio, where a crowd of guests had gathered. She hung back, her eyes moving from face to face. They were all strangers to her, a crowd of young people, expensively if casually dressed, all with an air of innate self-confidence that comes from having plenty of money in the bank and from having attended all the right schools.

Eventually, a little apart from the rest, Andrea sighted her husband's tall figure. He was handing Cecile a drink, his head bent to hear something she had said, his whole attention concentrated on his glamorous companion. Andrea's heart contracted with pain. Not for the first time, she pondered whether he and Cecile had been longtime lovers. But then why had he not married Cecile?

Standing still and unnoticed in the shadows, she tried to push aside these fruitless thoughts, but all that came to replace them was an aching sense of ostracism. The cliché that you could be loneliest in a crowd was a true one, as she now discovered; she had felt more at peace on her solitary walks along the mountain trails than she did now, surrounded by this animated, uncaring group of strangers. She glanced down at the friendly bulk of the trees, and there, among the shining lanterns, she saw a familiar face. It was Clayton. Edging around the couples on the patio, she ran across the grass towards him, just as, many years ago, she had run to her father with her scraped knees and broken toys. 'Clayton!' she called.

He straightened from tending the barbecue coals, wiping the palms of his hands down the sides of his levis. 'Why, hello there, Andrea,' he said, and with his usual directness added, 'What's wrong?'

'Oh, nothing. Everything. I don't know.' She laughed deprecatingly at her own incoherence. 'I'm glad to see you. I don't know anyone here.'

Clayton refrained from asking Stuart's whereabouts; perhaps he had already seen him with Cecile. He said easily, 'Charcoal's about ready. There's enough grub here for a small army. Hope that gang up there is good and hungry!'

Under the trees Andrea now saw long tables heaped with

tossed salads, aspics, rolls, and platters of sliced ham and
turkey for those who did not want steak. Her rebellious
stomach churned at the sight of so much food.

Unaware of her problem, Clayton casually uncovered a
great pile of steak. 'T-bone and filet,' he remarked. 'Nothing but the best.'

Andrea bowed her head, fighting down a surge of sick-
ness; but it was a losing battle. She whirled and fled up the
hill, even in her extremity remembering the way to the side
door. Down the hall to the bathroom . . . she pulled the door
shut and in spasm after spasm lost everything she had
eaten that day. Finally the convulsions ceased. She pulled
herself upright, and splashed cold water on her paper-
white face, holding on to the edge of the counter for
support.

'Andrea! Are you okay?'

'It's all right now, Clayton,' she said, her voice hardly
audible. 'You can come in.'

He caught her with firm and comforting hands as she
swayed towards him. 'Easy there, easy,' he soothed. In the
same slow drawl he suggested, 'Did you ever think you
might be expecting a baby, Andrea?'

Utterly aghast, she looked up at him, brown eyes huge in
her drawn face. 'Oh, no, I couldn't be——'

'You sure have all the right symptoms. Besides, it
wouldn't be any great tragedy, would it?'

Her head was resting against Clayton's shoulder; her
lashes drooped shut. Her initial reaction was a rush of pure
joy that within her she might be carrying Stuart's child, a
baby they had created in love and passion. But almost
immediately her happiness was shot through with pain,
because Stuart, the father of the child, no longer loved her.
Even worse, he might not believe the child was his, since
he was convinced she had been unfaithful to him . . .

'I can't be pregnant,' she murmured, wishing she could
believe her own words, and avoiding Clayton's shrewd blue
eyes. 'I'm overtired, that's all. I'll go and see a doctor soon,
I probably need some iron pills or something like that.'

'Well, whatever you say,' Clayton replied, patting her on

the shoulder as though she were a nervous filly. 'But make sure you do hike yourself to a doctor, I don't like——' he broke off as the door was pushed open. Stuart's big frame filled the doorway, his eyebrows drawn together in an angry frown.

'What the hell's going on here?' he demanded.

Because her mind was still grappling with the suspicion Clayton had planted there, Andrea could not meet her husband's eyes; a guilty flush stained her cheeks.

'I've been looking for you everywhere,' he continued furiously. He switched his attention to Clayton, saying, 'Cecile wants the steaks started. You'd better get out there.'

'Take it easy,' Clayton said softly, not releasing his hold on Andrea. 'Some things are a little more important than Cecile Martin and her barbecue.' For one horrified instant Andrea thought Clayton was about to reveal what they had been talking about. She made a tiny sound of protest, which neither man noticed.

'What do you mean by that?' Stuart asked with dangerous quietness.

'I mean your wife. She's just been very ill. I'm going to take her home, this is no place for her right now.'

'Ill?' Stuart repeated. Andrea could feel his eyes boring into her, but kept her lashes downcast, frightened by the conflict that was developing between the two men who had been comrades for so many years. And so she missed the startled concern in Stuart's eyes.

'Yeah,' Clayton drawled. 'You tell Miss Cecile I'll be back in half an hour. None of the guests will starve in the meantime, I don't imagine.'

'I'll take Andrea home,' said Stuart purposefully.

'Clayton can take me,' Andrea interjected, wary of her husband's air of pent-up irritation.

'You're my wife and my responsibility—so I'll take you home.'

'But you know how much you wanted to come to this party, Stuart,' Andrea argued, hearing her unruly tongue go on. 'Besides, I'm sure Cecile is depending on your company.'

His lips tightened ominously, and again her eyelids fell. Speaking to the older man, Stuart said, 'Look, thanks for your help, Clayton, but I can drive Andrea home. Give Cecile my apologies, will you?'

'Okay, you're the boss,' Clayton said agreeably. He gave Andrea one last pat on the arm. 'Take care of yourself; you'd better stay away from the horses for a couple of days until you're feeling better.'

She gave him a grateful smile. 'Thanks, Clayton,' she said softly, sure he would understand she was thanking him for keeping her secret. With a quick conspiratorial wink in her direction, Clayton disappeared to look after the barbecue.

'Wait here,' Stuart said formally. 'I'll get your jacket.'

Trying not to think about anything at all, Andrea washed her face again while he was gone, deploring its ghost-like pallor. When he came back, he led her along the hall to the front door. He passed her the jacket. 'Here,' he said, 'you'd better put this on if you've been sick. I wouldn't want you to catch cold.'

Andrea stopped in her tracks, making no attempt to take the proffered garment. 'What do you mean—*if* I've been sick?'

'My dear Andrea, you made it perfectly clear from the beginning that you didn't want to come to this party, and now, because of this very convenient illness, you're being taken home.'

'You don't have to take me home,' she interrupted furiously. 'Clayton offered to. And then you would have had Cecile to yourself, with no wife around to spoil your fun.'

His brows contracted. He opened the car door and said unceremoniously, 'Get in. If we're going to argue, let us at least do it in privacy.'

She sat stiffly in her seat as the Mercedes purred down the driveway and on to the main road.

'All I was trying to say,' Stuart went on smoothly, as though there had been no interruption, 'is that this illness was rather too opportune—I never did have much faith in coincidences.'

However, in the intervening few minutes, Andrea's brief anger had burned itself out. 'It's useless for me to argue with you,' she said wearily. 'You never believe a word I say, anyway.' She stared pointedly out of the side window, her hands folded neatly in her lap, and the rest of the journey was accomplished in strained silence.

When they arrived home, Stuart was the first to speak. 'I'll take you upstairs. Would you like me to bring you something to drink?'

She glanced up at him, hoping to discern even a trace of concern on his face, but it was as withdrawn and inscrutable as ever. Since the last thing she needed now was a tête-à-tête with her husband in their bedroom, she said coldly, 'No, thank you. And I can manage on my own.'

His mouth twisted to an ugly line. 'You really don't need me for anything, do you, Andrea? Then perhaps I will go back to the party. At least there I'll be treated like a human being.' He slammed the door behind him, and Andrea heard the car engine start up, and the roar of the motor diminishing down the driveway.

Trying to block out his last cruel words, she was almost grateful to be alone, so that she could finally allow Clayton's suspicions about her state of health to crowd back into her mind. Pregnant, she thought in wonderment ... Stuart's baby. But then, panic-stricken, she wondered how she would ever cope with this new complication. Her body had trapped her in a predicament as old as time; it was inevitable that sooner or later Stuart would find out about it. She smiled to herself mirthlessly. Pregnancy was certainly one secret she could not hide from him for long.

In the bedroom she undressed slowly, trying to decide what should be done. After all, there was no point in getting in a panic, when it might prove to be a false alarm, a reaction possibly caused by the intense mental strain of the past month. The obvious solution was to consult a doctor and discover the truth about her condition. The question was, who ... the doctor in Valleyfield, whom she had met when he had visited the ranch one day, was a personal and longtime friend of Stuart's, so he was eliminated automatically. If only she could go to Calgary, she thought, where in the anonymity of a big city she could consult a stranger whom she need never see again. Calgary—that was the answer. She would ask Stuart for the car, tell him she had some shopping to do—more deception, but it couldn't be helped.

With this decision made, she was able to sleep, although some time later in the night she awakened to hear the Mercedes drive past the house to the garage. The little bedside clock said two-thirty. Fighting back jealousy at the thought of Stuart and Cecile together for all those hours, Andrea lay still on the far side of the bed, and pretended to be asleep when Stuart entered the room.

The next day she was with the children in the stables when Stuart joined them. 'I'd better go for a ride with you two right now, because tomorrow I have to go to Calgary,' he said to the twins. 'Let's take the trail up to the look-out at Aspen Grove, I think you can manage that ride nicely now.'

Andrea's ears had pricked at the mention of Calgary; she had rather dreaded the idea of fighting the city traffic on her own, but now she could go with Stuart—one problem solved. So while the three of them were riding, she phoned for a doctor's appointment, and when she and Stuart were drinking their after-dinner coffee in the sunroom, she said, 'I'd like to go with you to Calgary tomorrow, Stuart, please.'

'I'm just going on a business matter, Andrea, there's no need for you to come.'

She had not anticipated any opposition; remembering the appointment she had already made, she persisted, 'I won't bother you. I have some shopping I'd like to do.'

He scowled at her. 'Couldn't it wait until another time?'

No, she thought silently, it couldn't. 'What's wrong?' she demanded. 'Why don't you want me to go? Are you meeting Cecile there?'

He sighed with exasperation. 'No, Andrea, I am not

meeting Cecile there. I *was* rather hoping for a day away from all this eternal arguing. But if shopping is that important to you, you'd better come. I'll be leaving around nine.'

She hoped her relief was not too obvious. 'Thank you,' she said coolly. 'I'll go and tell Maggie, and I'll give Clayton a call to see if he can take the twins riding tomorrow.'

Ordinarily Andrea found the city stimulating, a pleasant change from the placid life of the ranch. But there was too much on her mind on this particular visit. With scant ceremony Stuart let her off at one of the main intersections downtown. 'I'll meet you at the hotel at four-thirty,' he said. 'Don't be late, I want to be home in time for dinner.'

He pulled out into the street; the heat beat up from the pavement, and the crowds that thronged it jostled and pushed her. She watched the car until it disappeared in the mêlée of traffic, oddly hurt that he had not even suggested meeting her for lunch. Surrounded as she was by concrete and steel, by noise and confusion, by innumerable people, she felt very much alone. Then she gave herself a mental shake, for her appointment was in ten minutes and she still had two blocks to walk.

The doctor's office, on the tenth floor of a brand new medical complex, was quiet and pleasantly furnished with a décor of soft blues and greens, attractive seascapes on the walls. Andrea thumbed through the pages of a glossy magazine as she waited, not really taking in its contents. All too soon the receptionist said, 'Dr Highsmith will see you now, Mrs Trent. This way, please.'

The doctor himself, silver-haired and immaculately groomed, had a reassuring twinkle of humour and kindness in his eyes. In a very short time he gave her his diagnosis. 'You're almost two months pregnant, Mrs Trent.'

Deep in her heart she had known this was what she would hear, and again, unbidden, came that swift surge of happiness. But close on its heels crowded a multitude of fears, centred on the enigma Stuart had become: what would he feel about this, loathing her as he now did?

As though the doctor had read her mind, he advised,

'You must take better care of yourself, Mrs Trent. This isn't a time for anxiety or strain, you know.'

She smiled at him weakly. 'I will,' she promised.

'You don't want to believe any of the old wives' tales about the peril of childbearing,' he added, aparently interpreting her lack of enthusiasm as fear. 'Having a child, especially your first, is a unique and beautiful experience.'

Only if your marriage is a happy one, she thought, bitterly resenting the fate that now deprived her of sharing the news of her unborn child with her husband. As she descended the elevator to the ground floor, she found herself terrified by the prospect of facing him later this afternoon, now that her suspicions had been confirmed. Although briefly she considered the possibility of telling him the truth, she knew she didn't have the courage.

Unable to remain still, yet with no destination in mind, she started walking, automatically threading through the noonday crowds, obediently waiting for the 'walk' signal at the traffic lights. Although her panic gradually abated, coherent thought still seemed impossible, and her mind was a seething jumble of contradictions: she could not tell Stuart about the baby, but she would have to sooner or later; she did not want to deceive him again, but she seemed to have no other alternative.

Into this maelstrom of confusion there suddenly dropped an image of the farmhouse in Cape Breton, with its rambler roses yellow against the old stone walls, its herb garden sweetly scented in the dusk, its apple orchard laden with scarlet fruit every autumn. Without consciously making a decision, she hailed a taxi and said crisply to the driver, 'Take me to the airport, please.'

Afterwards she would not be able to recall a single detail of the taxi journey; she must have been in a trance, all normal thought suspended, once she had succumbed to the overwhelming urge to flee from Alberta and the ranch and Stuart. Inside the terminal she soon discovered there was a flight to Halifax in three and a half hours with bookings still available on it. She sat down to wait in one of the padded leather seats, leaning back gratefully, for she was tired.

Time passed slowly. The scene in front of her was one of constant movement: travellers with suitcases, air hostesses, families, couples . . . with a sinking heart she gradually realised they all had one thing in common; they were moving with a sense of purpose, they knew where they were going and why. Whereas she herself was lost and drifting, without any clear goal in sight. Nor, she knew, would the familiar landmarks of her childhood restore her peace of mind. So what was she to do? A wave of the familiar dizziness approached and slowly receded.

'Are you all right, ma'am?'

Startled, she looked up. A middle-aged policeman was eyeing her with concern, his shrewd gaze assessing the understated elegance of her clothes and the mute unhappiness of her piquant face. She managed to smile. 'Yes, I'm fine, thanks. I forgot to eat lunch, that's all that's wrong.'

'There's a restaurant down the corridor, ma'am. Sure you're okay?'

'Yes. Thank you.'

The policeman walked away. More to fill the time than because she was hungry, Andrea ate a sandwich and drank a glass of milk in the cafeteria. Only half an hour before flight time . . . perhaps she'd better get her ticket. There was a line-up at the counter and she waited patiently, again with that strange sense of being in limbo. The family in front of her, a young couple with two small children, was also going to Halifax; finally it was Andrea's turn.

'Where to, madam?' asked the smartly uniformed girl, with a bright professional smile.

Andrea opened her mouth to ask for a one-way ticket to Halifax, but the words stuck in her throat. Where to? Where to, indeed? Was she going to follow in Barbara's footsteps, and callously leave Stuart alone again with his children? No matter what he had done, no matter how badly he treated her, she could not do that to him.

'Did you want to purchase a ticket, madam?' the girl

repeated, a faint edge of impatience behind her polite words.

Andrea said blankly, 'A ticket? Oh, no—no, I'm sorry, I've changed my mind. But please—what's the time?'

'Almost four-thirty.'

'I'll be late!' Andrea gasped. Ignoring the curious looks of the other passengers, she left the queue and began running towards the terminal's main exit. Signalling to the nearest taxi driver, she directed, 'The Castleburgh Hotel, please. And hurry!'

She sat on the edge of her seat in an agony of impatience; the rush-hour traffic had started and the taxi inched its way along the crowded streets. It was nearly six when they drew up outside the hotel. Quickly paying the driver, Andrea ran up the steps and into the lobby, this time not even noticing its baroque magnificence. There was no sign of Stuart. Breathless and distraught, she forced herself to look more carefully—he must be here. Surely he wouldn't have left without her?

'Mrs Trent?'

It was the doorman. Glad to see a familiar face, she smiled at him. 'Have you seen my husband?'

'He's in the cocktail lounge, ma'am. He was worried about you.'

'Thank you,' she said, wondering with a flicker of hope if this could be true—could Stuart have been worried about her whereabouts, concerned because of her lateness?

The dim lighting of the bar momentarily confused her; frowning, she peered into its murky corners. Then she saw Stuart seated alone at a table on the far side of the room, his back towards her. Conscious only of gratitude that he had waited for her, she hurried over to him and touched him lightly on the shoulder. 'Stuart?'

He turned so sharply that he almost upset his drink, half rising as he did so. Unmistakably, for the length of time between two heartbeats, his features were filled with a profound relief; she could not have misinterpreted it ... he was glad to see her. Eagerly she put her hand on his sleeve, the words, 'Stuart, I'm going to have a baby,' on the tip of her tongue.

But before she could say them, a mask of ice-cold antagonism descended over his face. 'Where the hell have you been?' he demanded. 'Couldn't you have telephoned the hotel to let me know you were going to be late? I thought you'd had an accident——'

'Would you have cared?' she interrupted bitterly.

'—or that you'd decided to leave me.'

This last statement was so close to the truth that Andrea was struck dumb, her heart like a stone in her breast.

Stuart made an obvious effort to control his anger. 'Do you want a drink?'

'No, thank you.'

'Come on, then. I reserved a table for dinner when I realised you were going to be late.'

Andrea let Stuart choose from the elaborate menu for her, and when the food arrived, discovered to her surprise that she was hungry.

'Where did you eat lunch?' Stuart asked, endeavouring to make conversation.

'At the——' she began, then stopped in consternation. 'At a little restaurant downtown somewhere,' she amended vaguely. 'I can't remember its name.'

'What did you buy?'

'Well—nothing.'

'I thought you came here to shop,' he accused.

'I couldn't find anything I liked.'

His eyes narrowed with suspicion. 'What *did* you do all day, Andrea?'

Like a cornered animal, her eyes huge in her thin face, she stared at him in total silence.

His voice sharpened. 'Did you meet Ronald? Is that what you did?'

She came to life. 'No!'

'Then where were you? Why can't you tell me the truth for once?'

'It's none of your business where I was,' she cried frantically. 'Why can't you leave me alone?'

'I might just as well,' he said heavily. 'Let's get out of here.'

The sun was setting as Stuart headed the car towards White Birches. As they left the city the road stretched before them like a golden ribbon, while the jagged outline of the mountains was pitch black against the pale evening sky. It was a view of incredible and haunting beauty, utterly remote from Andrea's emotional turmoil. Exhausted, she closed her eyes and slept.

CHAPTER SEVEN

THE day after the ill-fated trip to Calgary, Andrea felt more than usually tired, her body craving sleep. She picked at her breakfast, not really feeling like eating.

Maggie admonished her, 'Come now, Andrea, you must eat more than that, if you're to stay healthy. You're thin and peaked enough lately without dieting, my dear.' She gazed worriedly at Andrea, concern evident on her face. She had noticed Andrea's despondency since her return from New York, and she had sensed the tension that existed when Andrea and Stuart were together, no matter how carefully both of them attempted to disguise it. She asked tentatively, 'Is something bothering you, my dear? Have you not been well lately?'

'I'm all right, Maggie. Please don't worry about me.' Any further conversation between them was rendered impossible at that moment, to Andrea's relief, when Stuart joined them in the kitchen. Andrea knew he had already been up and working for a few hours, because she had heard him leave before daybreak; unseen in the darkness enshrouding her room, she had watched his long figure walk slowly away from the house to the stables. He had seemed so alone, so untouchable, so distant from her, in the grey mask of dawn, that she had wanted to run to him, to shatter the shield that he had erected between them. But she had not done so, knowing in advance that her action would be futile—he despised her for what he believed she had done to him.

Now he poured himself a large drink of juice and walked over to the table. His eyes, unrevealing in their grey depths, met hers and pondered her for a moment. As he sat down across from her, Maggie excused herself, leaving them alone.

'You're looking tired this morning, Andrea.' A toneless statement.

'Yes, I guess I am. I didn't sleep very well last night.' She tried to make a joke. 'I must be getting old—it takes me longer to get moving in the mornings lately.'

He was dressed in his levis and a checkered shirt, the sleeves rolled above his elbows, exposing tanned and muscular arms. Hot and dusty, he carelessly wiped the sweat from his forehead. 'Maybe you need a holiday away from the children for a while,' he offered.

'I didn't know you cared,' she snapped back, yet immediately regretting her sarcasm.

His expression remained the same, inscrutable and cold, as he changed the subject. 'That new charollais bull I bought yesterday should arrive today. It will be a valuable addition to the herd.'

Although she did not respond, he seemed not to notice, and went on talking about the bull and work on the ranch generally. His conversation and its tone were not unfriendly, betraying none of the ambivalence that she knew existed, but he was talking to her as he would a neighbour who had dropped by for friendly but superficial chatter. Her throat tightened with the threat of tears, and she struggled to prevent the visual evidence of these. Yet she was crying inside; Stuart, who had once been closer to her than the air she breathed, had become an uncaring stranger.

'I'm riding out to the western section to check fences.' He paused. 'Do you want to come?'

Andrea looked up quickly. Did she want to go with him? Oh, yes, she thought wildly, yes, she wanted to go; but then, remembering her secret, she forced herself to respond, 'No, thanks, I don't think so.' Her voice sounded hollow and empty to her own ears, nor could she think of an explanation for her refusal other than the truth. Since she couldn't tell him that, she said no more.

He looked at her and waited. Seeing that she intended to say nothing further, he asked, 'Why not?'

She had not expected him to pursue her for reasons. She

groped for words. 'Well . . . I can't really ride that well, and it's such a long distance.'

'Of course you can ride well enough. Clayton has told me how much progress you've made. We'll take it easy. Pack a lunch and let's go. As I said, you're not looking as well as you might, you need more fresh air. Besides, it'll give us a chance to be alone . . . and maybe talk a little . . .' He waited.

Andrea desperately wanted to accept this peaceful overture offered to her by Stuart; it was the only one he had offered her in weeks. But her need to hide her condition was equally desperate, and she was driven to abruptness. 'I said no, Stuart. I don't want to go.'

He flinched at the sharpness of her words, and she saw anger flare again in his grey eyes. 'So my company is that hard to take, is it, my dear wife? Do you prefer someone else's—Ronald's, for example?'

'That's unfair, Stuart! If you would only listen to me. I haven't seen Ronald since New York and you won't even believe the truth of that situation. I wish you would.' Her voice was a desperate plea. She was torn between the desire to go with him, to go anywhere with this man she had married, and the fear of doing something that might risk the life of their unborn child.

'Believe you!' He spat the words, his mouth harsh and unyielding. 'I have yet to meet a woman I could believe and trust. I should have remembered the lesson that Barbara worked so hard to teach me. Yes, she was a damn good teacher. And so are you, Andrea.' His words stung cruelly, so that tears glistened in her eyes. 'You learn quickly too, don't you, Andrea? Tears are the inevitable feminine weapon. You must soften my hardened heart with tears. Spare me the cliché, please.'

She could not speak. She felt as if he were physically striking her with these terrible accusations. 'Oh God, how you must hate me!' she sobbed.

He said coldly, 'As you're not coming with me, I'll go to the other pastures as well. I won't be back until late. I trust you'll find plenty to amuse you here at the ranch.'

He moved towards her but did not touch her. 'You're to stay here,' he ordered. 'And I won't have Ronald Martin anywhere near this place. I meant what I said about him. If nothing else, think of the children. Barbara has already left them a legacy they find difficult to forget, and I won't have that repeated.'

He was unaffected by Andrea's trembling figure, nor did he acknowledge her quiet but defiant response, 'I'm not like Barbara. I'm not!' He stared down at her without bothering to reply, and her voice became flat and lifeless. 'Are you going alone, then? Maybe Clayton will go with you?'

'It wasn't Clayton's company I was requesting, Andrea. I'm going alone. I'm quite capable of taking care of myself, thanks.'

Again Andrea watched her husband leave. He swung his lean body into the saddle and headed out across the field towards the tall stand of white birches, riding easily as if a part of the magnificent animal that carried him. A summer wind, warm and scented, rippled the surface of the tall grass through which he rode. Although he was strong and hard and totally masculine, Andrea knew there was a gentleness and a vulnerability beneath his terrifying strength and self-control. Somehow she had to break through to this tenderness ... if only she knew how!

The day dragged on, becoming hot and sultry. Andrea watched the children as they rode their ponies round the main house and in the adjoining fields, envying them their carefree attitude; they lived each moment with no thought for the past or the future, and were totally engrossed in the enjoyment and fun of their play.

Restless, and physically oppressed by the heat, she felt suffocated by her unhappy thoughts. Later in the afternoon she lay down, but neither sleep nor rest would come to her, and she tossed and turned on the damp sheets.

Finally she got up and went outside. Her gaze fell on the stand of white birches to the west, the direction in which Stuart had ridden that morning. The trees stood tall and still, etched against a darkening sky. With the two huskies bounding after her, she walked down the lane leading away from the house, and then through the tall grass of the field, feeling its sharp sting against her legs. Suddenly she realised that she and the two dogs seemed to be the only signs of life. No birds flew. The grass was motionless, unruffled by even the slightest breeze, and they were totally engulfed by an all-pervading silence. It was eerie standing there, everything around her sharply in focus, as if finely carved with an artist's knife.

For a moment Andrea was awed by the peace and beauty of it all, feeling as if she were standing on the edge of the universe. Then an ominous premonition crept into her brain. Something was wrong. It was too calm, too quiet. The earth lay still in an expectant hush, and there she stood, on the edge of the earth, waiting ... waiting ... but for what?

The silence was broken with shocking suddenness. With a sharp crack a jagged slash of white lightning imprinted itself on the black sky before her; and to her left from the lane she heard the thud of hooves and Clayton's voice shouting a loud warning. He galloped towards her, and pulled up his horse in a swirl of dust.

'Get back to the house, Andrea. Hurry!' he yelled.

'What's wrong?

'Hail—it's going to hail!' He reached down and swung her up behind him before she had a chance to protest or to ask further questions. Jolted and frightened, she clamped her arms around his waist. All she knew was that something dangerous was about to happen ... and that somewhere on the open prairie, Stuart was riding—alone.

'Clayton, Stuart's out there! He went this morning, by himself. What'll we do? How do we find him?'

'Don't worry about him, Andrea. He knows what to do. He'll be okay,' Clayton shouted back, and swiftly left her at the main house. The dark sky, filled with rolling black clouds, was streaked with slanted white. The calm gave way in an instant to a driving wind, then to a slashing white downfall. It was not like the sleet Andrea had known in Nova Scotian winters, tiny ice particles mixed with rain. It was July now, midsummer, and a murderous hail of inch-wide pellets was cutting the leaves from the trees and decimating the undergrowth. Nature had gone berserk with a violence she had never witnessed before. In Clayton's eyes she saw mirrored her own fear, and that he should be frightened, terrified her all the more. She cowered into the shelter of the porch.

But within five minutes the vicious storm had passed. It was followed by a heavy downpour of rain that pounded the earth, forming puddles in the dirt and melting the beads of white as though they had never been.

Without Andrea having a conscious awareness of it, foreboding implanted itself like a tiny seed in the back of her mind. She physically sensed a danger that had no form, no definition . . . a vague whirling mist . . .

As the rain gradually diminished in intensity, she turned to Clayton. 'It's getting so late, it'll be dark soon. Stuart should have been home by now.' She drew in a deep breath, trying to alleviate some of the tension building within her. 'I know something is wrong, I can feel it. Please, can't we do something?'

He looked at her, placing his gnarled and leathery hands on her slim shoulders. 'Easy, child,' he said softly. 'Believe me, he's a capable man, born to this country. He knows it like he knows his own soul. Don't fear for him, he'll turn up any time now.'

She nodded, desperately needing the reassurance of his words. But a nagging doubt remained with her, persisted and grew, until she felt that she would give in to panic. She was totally helpless. There was nothing she could do . . . but wait.

It was dark now. It had stopped raining and the sky was clearing. Small silver discs shone through scurrying clouds. The earth was quiet, hushed and still . . . not the same threatening silence that had preceded the storm, but a quiet that follows the release of a great tension.

The smell of the wet grass was sweet and fresh in Andrea's nostrils, as she walked alone near the stables. If only the peace and stillness that had come to the earth would come to me, she thought with some desperation. She was now convinced that something had happened to Stuart. The storm was over long enough for him to have left any shelter he had found and to have reached home. Clayton had returned to the bunkhouse, to check whether Stuart was there; in the meantime, Andrea waited, knowing that shortly she would go in search of Stuart, with or without the help of Clayton.

Then faintly in the distance she heard the rhythmic drumming of horse's hooves, steadily getting closer in the silver moonlight. She gripped the fence, her heart pounding in her breast. Thank God I was wrong, she thought to herself. Stuart's safe after all. But a few minutes later it was a riderless horse that broke through the darkness into her range of vision.

'Oh no! No!' she gasped, running to intercept Shah's mad gallop. The stallion stopped by the stables, winded and lathered, his coat streaked with rain and sweat, his sides heaving. Andrea spoke quietly to him, gently rubbing his soft muzzle with her fingers.

'Where is he, Shah? Where is he, boy? What's happened? If you could only speak ... if you could only lead us to him!' Then she saw the scraped and bleeding flesh over the stallion's ribs. Her eyes widened in fear, and for an instant her whole being cried out to Stuart, lost somewhere in the vast blackness of the night. But she fought and conquered her panic, knowing now that the uncertainty was over ... action was needed, immediate action. It was almost a relief. She led Shah into the stable and covered him with a blanket, then calmly and steadily walked towards the house.

The twins met her at the door. 'It's Daddy, isn't it? He's come home, hasn't he, Andrea?' They tried to push past her, to run and meet him, but she caught them both, kneeling and drawing them to her.

'No, it isn't your father. Shah came home alone.' She was not feigning the calm strength that emanated from her. 'But you're not to worry, we're going to look for your father and we'll be bringing him home safe.' She turned to Maggie, quietly asking, 'Please take the children into the living-room.' Then she walked purposefully into Stuart's study and phoned Clayton at the bunkhouse. 'Clayton . . . Stuart's horse came home alone. He's had a fall and he's cut and bleeding. We must go to look for Stuart—now!'

'I'll be right there,' he replied urgently. 'Get Maggie to call some of the neighbours, tell them what happened and ask them to join in the search. I'll organise the men down here.' He hung up abruptly. Within ten minutes he rode up to the main house accompanied by about a dozen men on horseback. 'Let's have a look at the stallion, Andrea.' She led him to the stables, where he examined the horse carefully.

'Did you say Stuart rode out to the western section?'

'Yes . . . due west,' she affirmed.

'Okay, we'll get started.' He patted her shoulder. 'Not to worry, child—we'll find him.'

'Let me come with you, Clayton. I can't stay here and be so useless. I want to help.'

'No, stay with the twins. They need you now. I'll keep you informed and I'll come and get you when we find him.' He said to one of the men, 'Pete, clean up this horse and rub him down . . . then join the search.'

Andrea turned to see Bruce and Heather, pale and obviously upset, standing behind her. 'I thought I told you two to stay with Maggie,' she chided, turning them in the direction of the house. 'Okay, you two, you heard Clayton—he's going to fetch Daddy. Now back home with you!'

'Oh, Andrea, it's so dark out. How will they find Daddy in the dark?' Heather quavered.

'They'll find him. I know they'll find him.' She took their hands and walked with them to the house. 'You two must help me make some cocoa and then it's to bed with you.'

The night wore on. The twins had finally fallen asleep, calmed by Andrea's reassurances. Riders came and went, but all had the same message—Stuart had not been found. At midnight Andrea was standing on the front veranda, leaning against the doorjamb, when she was joined by Maggie.

'Don't you think you should get some rest yourself, Andrea?' the housekeeper asked, making no attempt to keep the concern out of her voice.

'I can't sleep. It's useless to try.' Then the words came in a rush of released emotion. 'Maggie, if only I'd gone with him, like he wanted me to, this would never have happened. It's all my fault.' Tears welled in her eyes, making them bright with the terrible hurt she felt, bright with the painful belief that she had caused Stuart harm.

'Don't be silly, my dear. Accidents happen. You didn't cause this. And you certainly can't blame yourself for the weather.'

'Oh, you don't know. You just don't know.' Andrea fought the choking tightness in her throat, as Maggie shook her head sadly, unable to think of any comforting words to say to her. She, too, was fearful for Stuart's safety.

'You'd better get a jacket on, then, Andrea, it's getting cold out here.' She turned to go inside, but was restrained by Andrea's hand on her arm.

'You knew ... Barbara ... didn't you, Maggie?' The question was posed with a quietness that indicated a fear of the answer.

'Yes, I knew her. As well as anyone knew her, I guess. I'm not sure she even knew herself really.'

'What was it like for him ... with her?'

'Well, it must have been the nearest thing to hell on earth for anyone to live the way he had to with her. She never gave him any peace or joy ... not a single moment, to my mind ... from the time she first put foot in this house. He deserved better. He's a proud man and I think that's what kept him going; his pride would never let him break—his pride and those children of his. My, as far as he's concerned the sun rises and sets on them. No matter how hard he seems to be on them sometimes, I know that's the truth of his feeling for them. That's why he never left, even during the worst times, when she was here with those men, here in his own house—and one of them a neighbour of Mr Trent's too.'

Andrea caught her breath. 'What neighbour was this, Maggie?'

'Why, Ronald Martin, that's who. I don't know how that man had the nerve to come over here, especially after Barbara died ... with that sister of his, Cecile. And I don't know how Mr Stuart ever stopped himself from giving him the thrashing he deserved. I just don't know.'

Andrea asked no more but wandered down off the veranda, her thoughts and emotions a tangled mass inside her. 'Stuart thinks it's happening all over again,' she whispered to herself. 'He thinks I'm doing to him what Barbara did ... that I'm no different ...'

Dawn came slowly. A faint greyness tinged the sky, which gradually lightened. The air was chilly before the sunrise. Clayton rode in, his lined and haggard face revealing that he had had no luck in the search. He dismounted and walked towards Andrea, who had been sitting quietly, listening to the early robins sing. 'No news,' he said to her unspoken question.

'Oh, Clayton, if he's hurt and out there ...' she shook her head, terror blanking out thought. 'It was so cold last night.'

Clayton did not answer, but stared at the ground, pushing the toe of his boot back and forth in the dirt. They both looked up as another rider came in. To Andrea's consternation, it was Ronald Martin. No sooner had he dismounted than Andrea rushed at him, anger flushing her face.

'What are you doing here?' she demanded. 'Get out! You've done enough damage—you and your sister!'

His only response was a sneering half-smile as he said, 'Friendly as ever, aren't you, Andrea? As it happens, I was asked to be a member of the search party. And it would appear I'm the only one with any news.'

'News?' she gasped. 'What news?'

His mouth thinned vindictively. 'I hope you can handle being a widow, Andrea.'

She felt as though she had been struck. All the colour drained from her face as she gripped the iron railing of the veranda for support. 'What ... what are you saying, Ronald?' The words were torn from her. 'What do you mean?'

Clayton, in one step, grabbed the younger man and flung him violently against the wall. 'Yes, Ronald,' he demanded, 'what are you saying? What do you know? Answer me straight, or so help me, I'll——'

Ronald didn't wait for him to finish, muttering sullenly, 'I saw him, I found him.'

'Where? Damn you, talk!' Clayton's grip tightened and fear blanched Ronald's sharp features.

'By the old miner's cabin, by the river,' he blurted. 'He must have fallen over the embankment. I think he's ... dead.'

'No! He can't be!' Andrea cried. 'I would have known.' She covered her ears with her hands, muttering frantic words of denial over and over again.

Clayton let go of Ronald and turned to her quickly. 'Get hold of yourself, girl.' He shook her. 'Now calm down. We don't know yet if it's true ...' He didn't continue. Instead he called to Pete and Tom, who had just ridden into the front yard. 'Come on, we know where he is.' He ran towards his horse. Andrea looked up, having regained her control, and now knowing exactly what she was going to do.

'Wait, Clayton, I'm coming with you. Saddle the mare for me, while I get a jacket and some blankets.' After one look at her frozen face, Clayton did not argue.

'Go saddle the mare, Pete,' he ordered. Ronald moved towards his horse, as if to accompany them. 'No, you don't,' snarled Clayton. 'You're not coming. Stay away from her—from all of us—or so help me, I'll break your neck!'

Andrea ran down the steps to join them. 'I told Maggie to phone Doctor Grant,' she said breathlessly. 'He'll be here when we get back.' She mounted and the four of them rode out, straight west, through the tall grass, and past the stand of white birches ... to bring Stuart Trent home.

CHAPTER EIGHT

THEY rode at top speed, not sparing the horses or themselves, for almost an hour. Occasionally Tom and Pete, riding side by side, exchanged a low-voiced remark, but Clayton and Andrea travelled in silence, each absorbed in their private thoughts.

The trail was rough, flooded in spots from the rain, slippery with mud in others; it would have been totally impassable for any type of vehicle, and was treacherous enough even for the sure-footed prairie horses. Andrea was not even aware of the danger; time and space had lost their meaning, for her whole being was concentrated on one purpose, to find her husband. She guided Star with automatic skill, her body instinctively protecting itself from the worst of the jolts. To Clayton the strength of the love that Andrea bore for her husband became totally clear; here was a young woman whose resolve and loyalty could not be deterred.

They slowed their pace as the cabin came into view, and in spite of herself, Andrea's hands tensed on the reins.

'Over here, by the river,' Clayton directed, grim-faced and watchful. They rode for a few moments along the edge of the embankment, Andrea pulling slightly ahead of them. It was she who saw Stuart first, lying still and seemingly lifeless, by the water's edge. The river, swollen by the heavy rains, rushed through the gully, only inches from his body. She leaped from the mare, half sliding and half scrambling down the bank, an avalanche of loose rocks spilling after her. She knelt by his side.

On the long gallop through the early dawn light, Andrea had deliberately kept her imagination in check, refusing to anticipate what she might find at journey's end. The reality terrified her.

Stuart lay on his back, one arm outflung; the fingernails

161

were torn and broken and his hands ingrained with dirt as though he had been trying to crawl up the bank. One leg was twisted under him at a grotesque angle. The right side of his face was bruised and scraped, while his dark hair was matted with dried blood. She could see no evidence of breathing, no signs of life.

'Oh, no . . . dear God, no . . . he can't be dead . . . he can't be . . .' She covered her face with shaking hands, fear taking her in its icy grip again. Clayton fell to his knees beside her, placing his ear on Stuart's chest.

'No . . . he's alive, Andrea. He's alive.'

Unconsciously she was wringing her hands. 'What can we do? How can we get him back?'

Clayton did not answer, his skilful hands continued a rough-and-ready examination of the injured man. 'His leg's badly broken in a couple of spots; and I'd say he has some cracked ribs.'

'He's soaked, Clayton. And so cold,' Andrea stammered.

'Yeah. His heartbeat's pretty weak. We've got to get him home, as fast as we can.' He muttered an expletive, then called up the bank to Pete and Tom. 'Get the blankets and cut some limbs from the trees. We'll make a travois—it's the only way. We can't put him on a horse.' He lowered his voice. 'No telling how much damage there is internally. I only hope we're in time.' He turned to the figure kneeling beside Stuart.

'Stay with him, Andrea. I'll go and help them. I'll throw you down a blanket to cover him.' She nodded, not taking her eyes from Stuart's face.

She sat for a long time, cradling her husband's head in her lap, whispering softly to him, knowing that he could not hear her, but willing him to live, to hang on until they could get him to safety. 'I love you, Stuart,' she whispered. 'If only I'd come with you . . .'

Clayton returned. 'Easy, girl. We'll get him home in no time now. He'll be all right. He's a strong man, it'd take more than this to kill him.' But one glance at Clayton's face told Andrea that Clayton spoke these words without conviction; he looked desperately worried.

As gently as he could, he attached a temporary splint to Stuart's leg—but he was not gentle enough, because Stuart regained consciousness. Pain carved deep lines into his bruised face as his hands grasped at the rocks and dug into the dirt at his side.

'No ... no more ... oh, my God, please ...' His eyes, glazed and shiny, pleaded with his unseen assailant.

'Stop it, Clayton! Stop it! You're hurting him.' Andrea clutched at Clayton's arm, but he pushed her aside.

'We can't leave him here. We have to move him, there's no choice. Get out of the way, Andrea.'

Helplessly she watched as the three men eased their arms under Stuart's body and struggled up the bank. She breathed a prayer of heartfelt relief when Stuart lost consciousness again, his arms falling limply to his side.

The ride home seemed to last for ever. Andrea, on Star, rode alongside the travois, which Clayton had harnessed to Pete's horse. Stuart had been covered with blankets and made as comfortable as possible, his body firmly lashed to the tree limbs, but when he periodically recovered consciousness, Andrea could see how he was suffering from every movement of the crudely rigged stretcher.

Their progress was slow and tortuous, and it was nearly noon when they reached the main house. The children rushed towards them, breaking loose from Maggie's grip. Bruce stared at his father, his little face pale and fearful. 'He ... Daddy's ... is Daddy dead, Andrea?'

She pulled him to her quickly, and turned to gather Heather into her arms. 'No, Bruce, he's not dead.' She spoke with great gentleness, urging them towards the house as she spoke. 'He is badly hurt, though, and he's going to need our help. So come with me now and we'll let Dr Grant take care of him.'

It seemed an eternity, waiting, always waiting. Andrea tried to talk lightly with the children, endeavouring to hide the claustrophobic fear that engulfed her, but the tightness of her face and the tension that held firm grip on her entire body was obvious to all who saw her.

The door of the study finally opened, and Dr Grant

walked into the living-room. 'Can I speak to you, Andrea, please . . . maybe in the kitchen?' he requested gravely.

'Yes, yes . . . of course,' she said, moving quickly to lead him to the kitchen. She stood before him, hesitant and afraid to ask the question that was repeating itself in her mind. At last she uttered, a tremor in her voice, 'How bad is it, Doctor? Will he be all right?'

He looked at her, his eyes filled with concern, and spoke slowly, choosing his words with care. 'I'm not entirely sure just how bad it is, Andrea, and I won't be sure until we have X-rays taken. But I have to be honest with you. It doesn't look good. He was out there all night in the cold and rain, and right now he's running a high fever—there's a possibility of pneumonia. His leg is broken in three places; he's got several broken ribs, and severe facial lacerations.' He shook his head. 'It's just not good, Andrea. So I'm going to take him into the clinic in Valleyfield, that's the best place for him; I've ordered an amublance, it should be here any minute.'

For the first two days that Stuart was in hospital, Andrea stayed almost constantly at his bedside, pushing herself beyond her normal human limits. The hours were long and wearisome, filled with worry that Stuart might not survive this terrible assault on his body. All too often he moaned in delirium and pain, his broken voice pleading for peace and relief, until one of the nurses would give him an injection and he would sink into a sedated sleep.

After Andrea had gone more than thirty-six hours without sleep herself, the strain became more than she could bear. She left Stuart's side and stumbled blindly down the corridor, tears streaming silently down her cheeks. Not looking where she was going, she walked into the waiting room and over to the window, leaning her forehead against the cold glass pane that overlooked the clinic's main entrance. Her slender shoulders shook with suppressed sobs.

'Andrea! What's wrong?' It was Clayton. The expression of dread in his eyes told her only too eloquently what he was thinking. 'Is it Stuart? He isn't . . .?'

'Oh, no! No!' she wept now, almost uncontrollably.

'He's still alive, but it's been nearly two days, and there's no change, and it goes on and on. How much more can he take? He's in such pain. And I think at times I must be mad and that all this is surely a nightmare ... but it isn't ... and I'm not sure I can take much more, Clayton ... I'm so afraid that ... that he won't make it ... I'm so afraid ...' She turned her pale, tear-stained face to look at him as he gently put his strong arms around her.

'Mark my words, Andrea, he'll live. He'll walk out of here. I've no doubt of it. He's strong—and he's a survivor.'

'Oh, Clayton, he has to, he just has to,' she stammered. 'You were right, you see—I am going to have his child. He has to live to see the baby. And I couldn't live without him, Clayton, I love him so.' She had finally said it; she had told someone the secret that she had kept so carefully hidden.

'So, you are with child. I thought so, remember? Well, that news is bound to start Stuart on the road to recovery. And I know, child, just how much you do love him. But you've got to keep calm and take care of yourself, it won't help matters for you to get ill now.'

Reassured, Andrea felt better. She wiped her red and swollen eyes. 'But you won't tell him, will you? I must be the one to tell him.'

'Don't worry, my girl,' he smiled down at her, 'I wouldn't steal your thunder! Come on, let me take you for a bite to eat. It'll do you good to get away from here for a while.' His arm on her shoulder steadied her, and his calm strength helped her to regain control.

She returned to the clinic after lunch and quietly entered Stuart's room. Instantly, she knew that there was a change in him. He was no longer restless, his long body lying much quieter now, but his pyjamas were soaked through and his face glistened with beads of sweat. The fever had finally broken. With a start she saw that he had turned his head and was staring at her with glazed eyes. In barely audible tones he whispered hoarsely, 'Andrea, my Andrea ... you did come to me, after all ... you ...' Speech was obviously difficult for him—his words were slurred and uneven. He weakly reached out for her, and she placed her small thin

hand on his. 'Don't leave me, Andrea. Please ... stay ...'
His eyes closed, as if even these few words had been too
great an effort, and then he was asleep, still clasping her
hand.

'I won't leave you, Stuart. I promise I'll stay with you.'
She breathed a sigh of profound relief and gratitude. He
was going to get well. And he had wanted her to be with
him ... perhaps, just perhaps, his love for her was still
alive.

She was called back from her reflections by Doctor
Grant's gentle voice. 'Andrea, please come outside. I want
to talk to you.' She followed him out of the room, where
Clayton was waiting too. 'I've asked Clayton to take you
home. The worst has passed, and Stuart's going to be all
right. Now it's you who needs some careful attention.'

'No, I can't leave him. I promised I would stay.' She
turned to go back into the room, but was prevented by a
firm hand on her arm.

'You must do what I say,' the doctor said authoritatively.
'It will do Stuart no good if you make yourself ill, and
that's what will happen if you continue in this way.' He
paused and then added, 'Stuart will sleep a lot the next few
days and he's still very heavily sedated. He won't even miss
you. Besides, the children have need of you too, Andrea.
Take her home, Clayton, and that's an order.' With that he
walked away from them.

Andrea allowed herself to be led from the clinic to the
car. Yes, she was tired, so very tired, she thought. She
leaned her head back on the seat, enjoying the warm
breeze that blew her hair about her face.

They arrived home just as the children were finishing
supper. After soothing their anxiety about Stuart, Andrea
got them ready for bed, and then went upstairs to her own
bedroom. She stood for a long time in the jet of hot water
from the shower, relaxing gradually as the droplets flowed
over her weary body. Within moments of easing herself
between the cool silken sheets, she was lost in sleep.

She slept heavily at first, then fitfully, waking long
enough to gaze into the shadowed darkness that filled her

room and to reach out for Stuart—only to remember the reason for his absence. Early in the morning, when the room filled with a dim grey light, she heard children's voices from outside somewhere, but she had neither the energy nor the ambition to fully awaken. Instead she drifted back to the delicious inertia of sleep. And so it was nearly noon before she finally got up.

Later in the afternoon she drove into Valleyfield alone, having decided to wait and talk to the doctor before bringing the children to see their father. Stuart was awake when she quietly slipped into his room. He lay very still, but his eyes were sharp and clear. He seemed fully aware of his surroundings ... and of Andrea. She walked softly towards him, her heart pounding with the unutterable joy of knowing that he would live and be well again; joy also in the knowledge that he had wanted her by his side. Perhaps she would tell him now, today, about the baby. What greater gift could she give him? she thought.

She held a single talisman rose in her hand, a rose like rust-coloured velvet. Holding it out to him, her hand trembling, and her voice slightly husky, she managed to say, 'It's for you, Stuart, I thought you'd like it. It's so beautiful and so perfect.' She could not continue. Tears misted her vision, but she saw his hand reach out and touch the soft velvet petals of the flower.

'Yes, it is beautiful, very beautiful, Andrea.' He looked at her in a way that she could not understand, his eyes grey depths of immeasurable feelings that she was at a loss to interpret. 'But it's not perfect, nothing is perfect.' He paused, still looking at her as if trying to see to the very depths of her soul. 'This beautiful flower, so nearly perfect, as you say, also has thorns ... thorns that can cut deeply.' He withdrew his hand, adding coldly, 'You could probably get the nurse to put it in water—she may like it on her desk.'

His words tore at her, as the thorns of the rose would tear, and unbelievingly she watched the cold and distant look again invade Stuart's eyes, his face becoming a mask of hardened features. So he had not forgiven her for what he believed she had done, she thought numbly. He would never forgive her . . .

As they talked briefly and impersonally about the children and White Birches, Stuart's weakness was made obvious by the fact that he had to pause and rest often during their laboured conversation. A nurse joined them, brimming with brisk efficiency, bringing Stuart's supper tray.

'Perhaps you could help our patient with his meal, Mrs Trent, and then I'm afraid I must ask you to leave. Your husband is still very weak and too many visitors too soon can be detrimental to his recovery. I'm sure you understand.' She left as quickly as she had arrived. And as if to answer the question forming in her mind, Stuart added tiredly, 'Cecile was here just before you came.'

Andrea steeled herself to show no reaction to his statement, although inside she was screaming with hurt and frustration. 'Let me help you with your supper.' Her own words hung in the hollow air. But her help seemed to be more of a hindrance to him, and he wearily pushed her hand away.

'I can do it myself. I don't need your help. I don't want it anyway.'

But she persisted, 'You have to eat, Stuart, if you're to regain your strength.'

He turned on her, anger glinting in his eyes. 'What's the difference? What does it really matter to you, Andrea? You've got Ronald to fall back on, if anything happens to me. Maybe it would have been easier for you both if I had died out there. In any case, I'm sure he's been a tower of strength for you during these trying days.'

She gazed at him, the pain and utter confusion he was creating in her obvious in her face.

He added roughly, gripping her wrist, 'I'll be home soon, and by God, he'd better not show his face at White Birches! You can tell him that. I know it's been very convenient for you both, but I shall have to interrupt by returning to *my* home and *my* wife. Now get out of here—I'm tired, too tired to talk any more.' The muscles in his face tightened. He added hoarsely, 'I don't even want to look at you.' He turned his face away from her and closed his eyes.

Her gaze fell on the talisman rose on the table by his bed; its petals were already drooping. She had never felt hatred for anyone before, but for one brief, terrible instant, she was pervaded with bitter resentment towards Cecile, who was so wantonly wrecking Stuart's marriage; Cecile intended that there be no possibility of a reconciliation between Stuart and his wife.

On leaden footsteps Andrea left the hospital room, leaving the man she loved so desperately and so futilely, wondering how much longer she could survive the see-sawing of her emotions from hope to despair. At this moment all she knew with any certainty was that she had to get away from the clinic, go home to White Birches, and be alone for a while.

Andrea parked the car and slowly walked towards the clinic. Stuart was coming home to White Birches and she had driven into Valleyfield to pick him up, scarcely knowing whether she was glad or sorry to do so. She thought back over the strain, both mental and physical, of the past few weeks. Stuart had been unrelenting in the barrier he had once again erected between them. Nothing she could do could reach him, or satisfy him, and his bitterness towards her seemed to overflow into what should have been neutral conversations. He had come to hate her, to regret their marriage, of this she was sure now. But she could not leave him, not while she had even the slimmest chance of repairing their relationship. And besides, he, for some reason, had indicated again that he had no intention of letting her go.

She walked along the polished corridor to his room, her shoes echoing her footsteps. He was standing by the window, dressed and waiting, leaning heavily on crutches.

'What kept you?' he enquired sharply. 'I expected you an hour ago.'

'I'm sorry, Stuart, I was busy with the children. They're really excited that you're coming home—and they've been giving Maggie a merry chase this morning. Are you ready now?'

'Yes, of course I am. I said so, didn't I? I've already checked out.' He turned awkwardly, his jaw muscles tightening, a flicker of pain crossing his face. 'Let's go.'

Andrea picked up his suitcase, held open the door, and followed him down the hallway to the entrance. They said their goodbyes to the nurses and to Dr Grant, who promised to drive out to White Birches later in the week. She was tense and jittery and her heart ached for Stuart, who was obviously struggling with his handicap. Putting the suitcase down, she opened the car door for him.

'Here, give me the crutches. Hold on to my arm and ease yourself in.'

His face was ashen grey and dotted with beads of perspiration. 'Don't touch me, Andrea,' he snarled. 'I can manage. I don't need your pity or your help. Remember that . . .'

Searing desperation engulfed her, as she wondered how they could continue their marriage in this way. They would destroy each other if it went on like this. With his words ringing in her ears she did not venture to speak to him again, not sure that there was any safe subject between them now. He sat stiffly, staring ahead at the road that stretched before them. It was a beautiful day, hot and sunny; deliberately Andrea concentrated on the task of driving and on admiring the countryside around her—the mountains rising clean and strong, and the gently rolling foothills unfolding before them. At least, she thought, there is some peace and strength and comfort for me in this land. She had come to love it, perhaps as much as Stuart did.

When they reached the main house Andrea did not attempt to help Stuart from the car, knowing that any offer of assistance would be greeted with open contempt and a sharp refusal. She tried to ignore his struggles by immediately getting the suitcase out of the trunk. Heather and Bruce ran excitedly to meet their father, but he was unable to bend and hold them.

'Easy does it, children—your dad doesn't need your rough handling today,' warned Maggie. 'Glad you're home safe and sound, Mr Stuart. We all missed you a lot. Things'll get back to normal here now.'

'Thank you, Maggie.' He paused slightly, drawing in a long breath, as he awkwardly manoeuvred himself on the crutches. 'It's good to be home again, believe me, safe if not yet entirely sound.' He turned to look at Andrea, but she, without casting a backward glance, had swiftly preceded them into the house.

In the days that followed Stuart's return to White Birches, Andrea threw herself into housework and the children's activities—anything that would prevent her from dwelling on the steadily worsening situation that existed between her and Stuart. His moods were now totally unpredictable—she could never foresee how he would react to any statement or action of hers. At times it seemed that he was driven by some knowledge or secret of his own, one that he would share with no one. He no longer slept with her, but had asked Maggie to prepare the guest room, a room adjoining theirs, ostensibly so as not to disturb Andrea's rest. He tried to show an interest in the twins, but more and more he sought the solitude of his study.

The only times that he appeared to be at all relaxed were when he was visited by Cecile. These visits, as far as Andrea was concerned, were all too frequent. Ronald, needless to say, had not returned to White Birches since the night of the accident; unfortunately, through Cecile, he still managed to make his presence felt.

One evening after a hot mid-August day Cecile appeared again at White Birches. Andrea had just returned from having driven Heather and Bruce to Calgary where they were going to spend a few days with schoolmates. In the coolness of dusk, she was working in the garden when she saw the yellow Jaguar drive up to the front of the house. She went to meet Cecile, but could find nothing to say.

'Good evening, Andrea. It certainly was a beautiful day, wasn't it? I thought I'd drop in to see Stuart. He does seem to need cheering up lately, doesn't he? I thought perhaps

I'd take him for a drive, it would do him good to get away from this place.'

Still in silence, Andrea regarded Cecile's silky flowing dress of mint green, and her exquisite coiffure, made only too aware of her own dirt-smudged face, her dusty cut-offs and loose-fitting checkered shirt. Her feet were bare and she looked very young with her hair pulled back in pigtails. Cecile, on the other hand, exuded a sophisticated and elegant coolness.

'Where is Stuart?' Cecile persisted in a patronising tone.

'He's in his study, talking to Clayton.' Andrea moved as if to take Cecile to the study, but was stopped with a cool, 'Oh, don't bother, Andrea—I know the way only too well. You stay and tend your garden.' With this she turned and walked quickly and confidently into the house. Andrea, frustrated by her feelings of inadequacy and her very strong dislike of Cecile, went on weeding, jabbing at the soil angrily with her trowel, as she waited to see Stuart and Cecile leave together in the car. But to her surprise, ten minutes later Cecile emerged from the front door alone. She walked stiffly to her car, but then stopped, as though she had forgotten something. She turned, and approached the flowerbed where Andrea was working.

'Andrea dear, could I have a word with you?'

'What do you want, Cecile?' Andrea was tired and had no desire to talk with Cecile, nor did she attempt to hide this. And she was oddly frightened by Cecile's conciliatory tone.

'Look, I know how we feel about each other, but putting that aside, I think there are a few things you need to face—some cold, hard facts, if you want to call them that.'

'Get to the point, Cecile,' Andrea said impatiently.

'Well, dear, the point is this—why don't you give Stuart his freedom? You know how badly he wants it.'

'No, Cecile, I don't know how badly he wants it. He——' She was cut off by Cecile's spiteful response.

'Don't be a blind fool, Andrea! That he regrets his marriage to you must be more than obvious. Why don't you face it and let him go?' Her lips thinned, as the attempt at friendliness vanished. She continued ruthlessly, 'Stuart and

I ... we'll be together, never fear ... with or without a divorce. But things would be so much easier if you co-operated. You see, Andrea, he loves me, not you. It's I who satisfy his needs—*all* his needs——' She broke off, startled and a bit frightened by the anger on Andrea's pale face.

'Get out of here, Cecile. And don't come back! I don't want you near my home ever again. Do you hear me?' Andrea cried, through a mist of tears. She ran away from Cecile and entered the house, the blinding pain in her heart driving her to Stuart. She burst into his study, interrupting what seemed to be a somewhat heated discussion between him and Clayton.

Stuart turned on her, his eyes hard and devastating. 'What do you want?' He did not give her a chance to reply. 'I'm busy. I'll see you later. Now, get out of here!'

She whirled away from him, as if physically struck. In doing so, she slipped on one of the scatter rugs, lost her balance and fell against a chair, grazing her arm. Stuart reached out to her, but giving him no chance to help, she scrambled to her feet and ran sobbing from the room. In her wild flight, she heard Clayton's voice, clear and distinct with anger. 'You're a fool, Stuart Trent. Remember what I said to you a while ago? You're not the man I knew, and I don't think much of the one I see now.' A door slammed.

About an hour later, Stuart quietly entered Andrea's bedroom, struggling with the cumbersome crutches as he closed the door behind him. He stood watching her for what seemed like an eternity. Then he moved over to where she lay on the bed, her brown eyes huge. He reached out and lifted her chin with a gentle hand. She jumped at his touch, unable to understand the play of emotions on his face.

'Please ... don't ...' she stammered. 'I didn't hurt myself. I'm okay.'

'I know you didn't hurt yourself, Andrea. I did the hurting.' He spoke softly, cautiously.

Her heart was pounding. All she really wanted to do was to throw herself into his arms, to lean against his strong, warm body, to be held and comforted, and loved by him.

But she restrained herself, knowing that what he was feeling now was only guilt; he was sorry that he had caused her to fall, but he did not love her. No, what he felt for her was no longer love.

His fingers traced the smoothness of her skin, lightly touching her forehead, down the side of her face, to her lips. Her mouth went dry. How she wanted him! With all her heart and body she desired him. With a supreme and almost violent effort she pushed him from her.

'Don't touch me! Just don't touch me! I can't ... I can't ...'

He flinched, his breathing heavy. 'You can't what, Andrea? You can't stand my touch, that's what you're saying, isn't it?' His voice was husky and almost a groan. 'Am I so repulsive to you, then?' He stared down at the bedspread, as though memorising its pattern. 'Andrea, there's something we need to talk about. We have to talk *now*.' He turned to face her, seemingly gathering the courage to speak. 'Clayton spoke to me earlier today. He says ...' he paused, letting his eyes roam the length of her young body, looking for an indication of change. But the loose shirt she was wearing hid the slight thickening around her waist. 'He says that ... you're pregnant. Are you, Andrea?' His words were softly spoken, the strained control not only evident in his voice, but in his eyes and in his whole body. He reached out for her, taking her hand in his. 'Tell me,' he whispered.

She pulled her hand from his, her body tightening with fear. How would he feel about her now, with the added burden of a child from a woman he no longer loved? Her eyes flashed with desperation.

'No! I told him not to say anything! He promised he wouldn't say anything, that he wouldn't tell anyone—he promised. Oh, God, he said he wouldn't ...' The words were falling, tumbling from her. She tried to move away from Stuart, not really seeing him, but he stopped her sharply, his face pale and drawn.

'What are you saying, Andrea? What are you ... you didn't want me to know. Why? why?' He seized her, his hands holding her shoulders in a bruising grip. 'Why shouldn't I know, Andrea? I'm your husband—why shouldn't you tell me about ...' Then he paused and stared at her, the grey of his eyes darkening to an indefinable depth of black. 'The child, Andrea—' his voice choked, 'Is it my child—or is it Ronald's?'

She looked at him in shock and horror, stricken to her very heart that he could believe such a thing of her. 'Oh, Stuart ...' but she could not continue. The tears came in a rush, releasing her body from the tension that had built up over the past months. For a moment he did not release her, holding her firm in his grip. But suddenly he let her go, and she could see the dangerous storm of anger and hurt gather in his eyes, reflecting the conflict that shook the very depths of his soul. Then he slapped her, with a force that made the side of her face burn. Terrified, she lifted her eyes to look at him, as he stood towering over her. Her fingers touched the warmth of her cheek, red now with the imprint of his hand.

'You bitch! So you too prefer Ronald Martin. At least Barbara didn't go so far as to present me with the results of her liaison with him.' He pulled her roughly to her feet, drawing her body to his. His fingers wound themselves in her flowing dark hair. 'No wonder you didn't dare tell me. Does Ronald know yet?'

'Stop it!' she gasped. 'I can't take any more of this. Please——'

'I asked you if you've told Ronald!' he demanded, his face ashen grey and unrelentingly hard.

'There's nothing to tell him. The child is yours, Stuart. Why can't you believe me? I'm telling you the truth, I swear it!'

He laughed, his own voice grating and harsh, his eyes cruelly mocking. 'The truth, Andrea? You and the truth parted ways a long time ago. Ironic that I should at first believe you possessed so much honesty and innocence. Our whole marriage has been based on pretence and secrets. And you have the gall to speak of the truth!'

'You never listen to me!' she flared. 'You only believe what you want to believe. I don't know why, but you want to believe that I'm like Barbara—that I've cheated you as she did. Well, I haven't! And I'm sick of your accusations and your hatred and contempt. I can't go on living with you under these circumstances . . . I just can't go on like this . . .'

'And I'm sick of your deceitfulness, Andrea! I'm not a fool, whatever you might think. I *know* you're Ronald's mistress. Cecile told me——'

His words and their meaning exploded in her head. Her arm lashed out and she felt her stinging fingers and saw the red imprint of her hand on his face, a thin line of blood across his cheek where her ring had cut into his flesh.

He was dangerously close now, his eyes violent with an anger equal to her own fury. He reached for her, savagely drawing her to his hard body. 'Let's have at least one more charade before we call it a day, my dear Andrea.' Before she could flee, he lifted her and carried her to the bed.

She felt the passion and the desire rise in him, and guessed his intentions. But she did not have the physical strength to stop him; his mouth, rough and demanding, covered hers. She wrenched her lips free. 'No, Stuart! Please, not like this . . . not like this . . .' Tears of shame and hurt glistened in her eyes and on her flushed cheeks.

But he ignored her frantic plea. Darkness enveloped them both, and Andrea found herself wishing desperately that this sharing between them, which was now an act of hatred, could be one of mutual love. But there was no gentleness, no tenderness in Stuart. He was as harsh and demanding in his lovemaking as he had been in his accusations moments before.

Hours later, after they had lain together in the darkness, not touching or speaking, Stuart got up and left her. Before she finally fell asleep, Andrea made a decision, a decision that would change the course of her life. She would carry it out tomorrow.

CHAPTER NINE

TEN days had passed. And now, shaded by a silver maple from the afternoon rays of the August sun, Andrea sat in the garden of Cynthia's stately home in Halifax.

They had been days of transition and adjustment. At times the depths of the depression that had engulfed her had been almost too much for her to bear. After her arrival at Cynthia's, nearly every night she had awakened to sounds, strange in their newness, to find that their only existence was in her mind. She had felt shaken and broken at first, adrift in a sea of loneliness and desolation. But gradually she had gathered around her a protective covering of calm and detachment that was necessary for her survival. She vowed she would never again let anyone come as close to her as Stuart had been—never. She would live her life for her child, and no one else. She was determined to put Stuart from her mind—and from her life. And she struggled futilely with the impossibility of that goal. She would lie in bed at night, alone and frightened, yearning for Stuart's closeness and touch.

In the branches above her a pair of redstarts flitted; bees hummed drowsily in the beds of delphiniums and phlox, and against a white-painted trellis purple-blossomed clematis nodded in the gentle breeze. Within her, her unborn child moved, a tiny flutter that brought her mingled pain and joy. If only Stuart had wanted her, she thought—had loved her—they could have shared this miracle and the sharing would have brought them closer. But, as it was, the child could only be a burden to him, unwanted as she was unwanted. How could she have remained with Stuart, knowing that?

She leaned back in the lawn chair, her eyes closed, enveloped in the peaceful sounds and scents of a summer garden. And as so often happened, her thoughts went back to the day she had finally left Stuart's home . . .

Andrea had left White Birches the morning after that last terrible argument. She had stolen away, bruised and worn, but resolved not to perpetuate such a nightmare any longer. It seemed painfully evident that there was no possible resolution of the rift that divided her and Stuart, and that for Stuart's sake, as well as for the twins and the baby, her only choice was to leave. So she had gone early in the morning, encountering no one as she walked from White Birches out to the main road for Calgary. Even now she could remember the crisp clarity of the early morning air, with drifts of mist huddling in the hollows. The fields and trees were still silent, as if hushed by her defeat and final flight.

She sat alone on the bus, the journey passing in a blur of loneliness and emptiness; the conversations of people around her not penetrating her consciousness.

She could not remember the exact details of her flight to Halifax, for she had moved and breathed as if remotely controlled by a power beyond and outside of her. She had finally arrived at Cynthia's home, where she stood with proud straightness before her in the hallway. She could recall Cynthia's astonished greeting, 'Why, Andrea! What a surprise. And where is Stuart?' Then Andrea had not been able to conquer or control her emotions, not in the way that she had so carefully planned, but had collapsed in Cynthia's arms, the tears rushing forth all at once. She managed to say,

'I've . . . I've come alone . . . I've run away from Stuart, Cynthia.'

'You've left him? What foolishness is this? Come in, come in. And do stop crying, girl.'

Her aunt led her into a large, high-ceilinged living-room, not at all as gloomy and foreboding as Andrea had remembered. And Cynthia's acerbic lack of sympathy was the best thing for her.

'Now, child, what on earth is going on? Tell me everything from the beginning.'

Andrea began to explain, hesitantly at first, but later,

finding relief in talking to someone, she spoke more freely. 'And Cynthia, I'm pregnant, but . . .' her voice faltered, 'but Stuart doesn't believe it's his child. He believes . . . that Ronald and I . . .' She could not continue, but buried her face in her hands. 'I just couldn't stay. I couldn't. He hates me. And after everything he's been through, he deserves some happiness, too.' She paused and added brokenly, 'Maybe now he'll have a chance with Cecile.'

'With Cecile Martin? She'll never make Stuart happy, I can tell you that right now. And perhaps it's time you thought of what you've been through, instead of worrying about Stuart all the time.' Incisively her aunt continued, 'I'm going to phone him and tell him to get down here and fetch you home where you belong. It's time you both faced the truth.'

Horrified, Andrea expostulated, 'No! You can't—I won't let you. If you call him, I'll leave. I don't know where I'll go, but I'll walk out of the door and I'll never come back. I won't live with Stuart knowing that he doesn't love or want me. I can't live like that anymore! Promise me that you won't call him.' Seeing indecision on Cynthia's face, she pushed further. 'You must promise me, Cynthia. I mean what I say.' Reluctantly, Cynthia agreed.

The next day Andrea was deeply relieved that she had extracted this consent from her aunt. They had just finished dinner and had taken their coffee into the living-room when the telephone shrilled. Intuitively Andrea knew it was Stuart—looking for her, determined that she should live with him, no matter what their differences. She paled. But her voice was resolute when she said, 'If that's Stuart, I'm not here and you haven't seen me or heard from me. You promised, Cynthia. Please don't let me down?'

'Yes, I did promise, more fool me,' her aunt replied grimly. She picked up the phone. 'Hello? Why, hello, Stuart, how are you? . . . Andrea? No, I've not seen her . . . Oh, dear. Where else could she have gone? . . . Certainly, if I hear from her, I'll let you know. How are the twins? . . . I see. Please, Stuart, let me know when you locate Andrea, won't you? . . . Yes, all right. Goodbye.' The receiver was replaced with a decisive click.

'He sounds very worried,' Cynthia said mercilessly. 'And the twins miss you.'

Andrea winced. 'I miss them too,' she said in a low voice. 'But I can't go back.'

And there matters rested. Andrea had now been in Halifax for over a week, and the strain of her enforced separation from her beloved Stuart was beginning to show on her. Even so, she had come to deeply appreciate her aunt's particular brand of protective, if acerbic, affection. So she had been genuinely upset when the day before yesterday Cynthia had announced, 'My cousin Martha wants me to go to New York for a couple of days. You'll be all right on your own, won't you, Andrea?'

'Yes, of course,' Andrea said reluctantly, adding with sincere warmth, 'But I'll miss you.'

A faint pink colour stained Cynthia's cheeks. 'Nonsense!' she exclaimed. Nevertheless, Andrea could tell she was pleased.

So now Andrea was truly alone, for apart from a skeleton staff, the big house was empty. Perhaps that was why, this summer afternoon, she had sought the shelter and peace of the garden. Restlessly she got up from her chair and wandered aimlessly across the lawn, her fingers brushing the silken smoothness of the rose petals. She could not help remembering how Stuart had refused her gift of the talisman rose when he had been so ill. She wondered how he was . . .

She was leaning against a tree, watching two squirrels romp with animal agility on the grass, when she sensed a faint, almost imperceptible movement behind her. She turned. As though her thoughts had conjured him up, Stuart was standing there, his long body dappled with sun and shadow, his eyes intent upon her.

The world whirled. Without thinking or speaking she began to move away from him, her body tensing noticeably. He held out his hand to her, his voice softly pleading.

'Don't run away from me, Andrea. Please. We need to talk.'

Her body remained rigid, her face pale. Through wide, frightened eyes she watched him slowly approach her. He no longer used the crutches but walked with the aid of a cane. His limp was noticeable, although it did not seem to cause him any physical discomfort. Acknowledging her awareness of his limp, he said, 'It doesn't hurt much any more, except when I get tired.' He smiled, seeing that she was still poised for flight. 'But it has its drawbacks—I couldn't chase you if you decided to run.'

Still she did not speak. Her hands were clenched into tight fists at her sides.

'Oh God, Andrea, please. Don't be afraid of me. I won't touch you, I promise.' His voice broke. 'I won't hurt you—not again. Never again. Come and sit with me and let's talk.'

She felt herself being led to the garden bench, felt the strength and the careful gentleness of his hand on hers. She heard herself ask in a husky whisper, 'How did you find me? Who told you where I was?'

'Cynthia came to see me yesterday. She . . .'

'But that's impossible! She's been in New York for the last two days.'

'That's what she wanted you to believe. Cynthia knew you would never agree to her seeing me, and that you'd run away if you were aware of her intentions. But that's of no consequence now. The important thing is that I'm here—that I've found you at last.'

'You looked for me?' Her voice was tight and controlled, giving nothing away.

'Yes, I did look for you, Andrea. Do you think you're of so little consequence to me that I wouldn't? At first I thought you might have wandered off to the ranch. None of your clothes were gone . . . nothing. Then one of the ranch hands said he'd seen you walking towards the main road. I guessed then that you had left. I went after you—Clayton and I, that is—I couldn't drive very well with this leg. But you'd gone by then.' He closed his eyes, as if to blot out the remembrance of something. 'I searched everywhere. I even went to the Martins', to see if you'd gone there.' He felt her stiffen at this last statement. 'I know, Andrea, I know now that there was no reason for you to go there— no reason at all.' His voice revealed a terrible sadness.

She looked at him more closely, her heart throbbing wildly at the very nearness of him. How she longed to relax against him, to lean on him . . . just for a moment . . . to tell him the truth and depth of her feelings for him. He was thinner and his eyes held a haunted look. He breathed a deep sigh.

'I came to ask you to come home with me, Andrea.' He turned from her and ran his fingers through his mass of black curls. 'I want us to try to salvage something of this marriage. I——'

She did not allow him to finish, but rose quickly to her feet. 'No, I can't go back.' Her eyes, dark and glistening with tears, saw him flinch at her refusal, but that did not stop her from adding, 'I won't live with a man who hates me.' With that she ran from him, across the lawn, into the house, and up the wide stairway to her room. Deep sobs racked her body, as she fell across the bed. If only there was some escape—some end to the terrible pain that engulfed her mind and heart and body. How was she going to live without Stuart? How . . . when the very sight of him filled her with the truth of her all-consuming love for him?

A sharp knock sounded at the door. 'Andrea! Open the door. Open it, or I'll break it down.'

'No! Leave me alone . . . just leave me alone.'

'No, Andrea—I won't leave you alone. I came to talk to you, and that's what I'm going to do. Now open this door!'

Defeated, she lifted herself from the bed and went over to the door. 'It's unlocked,' she whispered.

He stood looking down at her tear-stained face. 'I told you I couldn't chase you—but I'll follow you wherever you go until you hear what I've come to say.' He took her hand in his, caressing her slim fingers. 'I have some things to say, and you're not to run away just because you think you know what they are. Do you understand me, little one?'

She nodded, waiting in almost unbearable suspense for whatever came next.

'Oh, Andrea, we victimised each other, and we let others, outside of us, create problems for us as well.'

'You mean Ronald and Cecile?' It was half question and half statement.

'Yes, I mean Ronald and Cecile.' His voice hardened. 'Their interference and plotting very nearly destroyed us,' he admitted, a tight sigh escaping, 'but only because I was fool enough to allow it.' He put a finger to her lips. 'Please don't say anything more until I try to explain; this isn't easy for me.' She could see that he was struggling with his feelings as he continued, slowly and carefully, 'If it wasn't for Cynthia coming to White Birches ... I don't care to think of the wasteful end of all of this. But now, at least we have one last chance, however slim that chance may be, after all I've put you through.'

Again he paused, his eyes dark with memory. 'After what happened to me with Barbara, I swore I would never re-marry, that I would never let any woman close to me, again. Then you came to me,' he smiled tenderly at her, 'and I knew immediately that I wanted you ... that my life was incomplete, only a kind of half-living, without you. But God help me, Andrea,' he muttered bitterly, 'living with Barbara I'd changed. I'd come to trust no one, man or woman. And you, who were closest to me, were to suffer the most from this. I . . .' he closed his eyes, his face show-ing clearly how difficult it was for him, '. . . I wanted to believe you—I wanted to desperately—but the fact that you didn't tell me things that seemed so simple and straightforward prejudiced me against you. Then there was what I thought I saw happening between you and Ronald in New York, and together with what Cecile told me about you two ... I just couldn't handle it, little one—I was nearly mad at the thought of losing you.' He swallowed hard, the muscles moving in his strong throat. 'And I didn't know what to do to hold you to me, so I ended up doing all the wrong things. I became caught in a trap of my own making, and I trapped you with me.'

'Stuart, I . . .'

'No, don't stop me, Andrea. I must say it all, then maybe

we can be finished with it. Cecile wanted to marry me, that was no secret to anyone. But, Andrea, I would never have married her—never. I don't love her—I've never loved her. There was nothing between us. Only in her own mind did the kind of relationship she described to you exist.'

Longing to express her joy at his words, yet still afraid that it was all too good to be true, Andrea murmured, 'I don't understand what Cynthia had to do with all this.'

He grinned, looking years younger. 'Cynthia can be a very formidable and persuasive lady, Andrea. As you know already, she didn't go to New York, she came West. Before coming to me at White Birches, she invaded the Martins' house—and it was an invasion! I guess the argument she had with Cecile and Ronald was something to see—and hear—I'm almost sorry I missed it.' A half-smile lit his face. 'I'm afraid I wouldn't have restrained myself in that showdown! Anyway, Ronald finally admitted to her that it was he who had made the advances, while you had done nothing but try to avoid him; you must really have hurt his pride. Cecile would admit nothing at first, but later indicated that she had lied to me and to you in the confrontation she had with you the day before you ... left White Birches. All that talk of divorce was totally untrue.'

He stopped speaking, but after a moment forced himself to continue. 'I ... what happened with Barbara, Andrea ... if you could only understand what it was like for me. She nearly destroyed me. She took everything I had—pride, honour, my name—and ground it in the dirt. But I was tied to her, chained by what I thought was my duty. You know, when I was lying in that gully with a broken leg, I could feel her presence, as if it were my ultimate destruction that she wanted, even after her own death.' He rubbed at his forehead with long fingers that were not totally steady. 'I did things to you that were so misdirected, my darling. They were the result of what Barbara had done to me— they had nothing to do with you, nothing.' His voice broke and she felt his body shudder violently. 'And I destroyed so much ...'

Andrea was crying openly, her small shoulders shaking

with the release of all the emotion that had been held in check for so long. Stuart gathered her into his arms, rocking her gently. She felt him wipe the tears from her face.

'There's a lot of salt in Nova Scotian tears, I'm told,' he said softly. 'Is that true? More salt in your tears than in mine, do you think?' She looked up at him. 'Yes, child, do you think I haven't wept bitter tears for the loss of you? Do you think I haven't suffered the tortures of hell, not knowing where you were or how you were. Knowing that you didn't want me to find you, that you didn't want to live with me any more. I knew that I'd driven you from me and had probably destroyed your love for me.'

For a moment he seemed drained and spent, unable to go on. She trembled with the wanting of him, the love and the hurt a confusing mixture in her mind. He bent over her, his mouth seeking hers. He kissed her gently . . . her eyes, her forehead, her face. His mouth lingered hungrily on hers and sought the very depth of her. He held her closely.

'Dearest Andrea, I love you so much, and I need you to be with me all the time. Without you there's no tomorrow, and no today. I can't live this way any longer. Now that I've found you, I can't let you go—ever again.' He clasped her tightly to the hardness of his lean body.

'I thought that . . . that you'd come to hate me,' she stammered.

'Hate you!' he exclaimed. 'Oh, Andrea, I love you more than my own life. I have no life without you. I'm nothing without you.'

Incredulous happiness flooded her entire being. 'And I love you too, Stuart. I love you so much,' she said, her voice shaking with emotion.

'Can you ever forgive me for the way that I've hurt you, little one?'

She held him tightly. 'Oh, Stuart, I need your forgiveness just as much. I've been so stupid and I've hurt you too. There are things I should have told you, from the start, but I didn't know how. Can you forgive me?'

'I think the time has come for us to begin again, my love,' he whispered softly.

Within her the baby stirred, startling her. She took Stuart's hand and placed it against her body, but the tentative fluttering movements had stopped.

'She's going to play hide and seek with us,' she said, lowering her eyes shyly.

'Ah, so our baby's to be a girl, is she? You have this on authority, do you?'

Andrea laughed quietly. 'No. I just know, that's all. I wanted you to feel her.'

'Don't worry, dearest. I'll be able to feel our daughter move and grow. We have time. We have tomorrow ... as well as today. Are you ready to come home with me now, back to White Birches?'

'Oh yes. I want to come home.' She hugged him to her. 'I want to be with you for ever and ever.'

'At least that long, my love. At least that long.'

In 1976 we introduced the first 100 Harlequin Collections—a selection of titles chosen from our best sellers of the past 20 years. This series, a trip down memory lane, proved how great romantic fiction can be timeless and appealing from generation to generation. The theme of love and romance is eternal, and, when placed in the hands of talented, creative, authors whose true gift lies in their ability to write from the heart, the stories reach a special level of brilliance that the passage of time cannot dim. Like a treasured heirloom, an antique of superb craftsmanship, a beautiful gift from someone loved—these stories too, have a special significance that transcends the ordinary. **$1.25 each novel**

Here are your 1978
Harlequin Collection Editions...

Original Harlequin Romance numbers in brackets

ORDER FORM
Harlequin Reader Service

In U.S.A.
MPO Box 707
Niagara Falls, N.Y. 14302

In Canada
649 Ontario St.,
Stratford, Ontario, N5A 6W2

Please send me the following Harlequin Collection novels. I am enclosing my check or money order for $1.25 for each novel ordered, plus 25¢ to cover postage and handling.

☐ 102	☐ 115	☐ 128	☐ 140
☐ 103	☐ 116	☐ 129	☐ 141
☐ 104	☐ 117	☐ 130	☐ 142
☐ 105	☐ 118	☐ 131	☐ 143
☐ 106	☐ 119	☐ 132	☐ 144
☐ 107	☐ 120	☐ 133	☐ 145
☐ 108	☐ 121	☐ 134	☐ 146
☐ 109	☐ 122	☐ 135	☐ 147
☐ 110	☐ 123	☐ 136	☐ 148
☐ 111	☐ 124	☐ 137	☐ 149
☐ 112	☐ 125	☐ 138	☐ 150
☐ 113	☐ 126	☐ 139	☐ 151
☐ 114	☐ 127		

Number of novels checked @
$1.25 each = $ _____
N.Y. and N.J. residents add
appropriate sales tax $ _____

Postage and handling $ ___.25___

                        TOTAL $ _____

NAME _____
            (Please Print)
ADDRESS _____

CITY _____

STATE/PROV. _____

ZIP/POSTAL CODE _____

ROM 2210

Offer expires December 31, 1978

And there's still *more* love in

Yes!

Four more spellbinding
romantic stories every month
by your favorite authors.
Elegant and sophisticated tales of
love and love's conflicts.

Let your imagination be swept away to
exotic places in search of adventure,
intrigue and romance. Get to
know the warm, true-to-life
characters. Share the special
kind of miracle that
love can be.

**Don't miss out. Buy now and discover
the world of HARLEQUIN PRESENTS...**

Do you have a favorite
Harlequin author?
Then here is an
opportunity you must
not miss!

HARLEQUIN OMNIBUS

Each volume contains
3 full-length compelling
romances by one author.
Almost 600 pages of
the very best in romantic
fiction for only $2.75

A wonderful way to collect
the novels by the Harlequin
writers you love best!